He leaned in close, as if to kiss her.

If she'd wanted to shove him away, she had ample opportunity. In no way was he forcing himself or taking advantage. She should have objected....

Instead she tilted her chin up, welcoming his kiss. When his lips brushed hers, a brilliant flash of white heat exploded behind her eyes and blinded her to common sense. A burst of passion surged, forceful and challenging. She wanted the kiss to deepen and continue for long, intense moments. She wanted to know his body in every sense of the word. Her ferocious need for him felt like nothing she'd experienced, as though they were meant to be together.

She had to be mistaken. The maid and the millionaire?

CASSIE MILES

MYSTERIOUS MILLIONAIRE

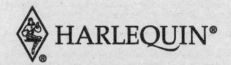

HARLEQUIN®

TORONTO • NEW YORK • LONDON
AMSTERDAM • PARIS • SYDNEY • HAMBURG
STOCKHOLM • ATHENS • TOKYO • MILAN • MADRID
PRAGUE • WARSAW • BUDAPEST • AUCKLAND

To those who love guitars and wooden boats.
As always, to Rick.

ISBN-13: 978-0-373-69315-3
ISBN-10:   0-373-69315-X

MYSTERIOUS MILLIONAIRE

Copyright © 2008 by Kay Bergstrom

ABOUT THE AUTHOR

For Cassie Miles, the best part about writing a story set in Eagle County near the Vail ski area is the ready-made excuse to head into the mountains for research. Though the winter snows are great for skiing, her favorite season is fall, when the aspens turn gold.

The rest of the time, Cassie lives in Denver where she takes urban hikes around Cheesman Park, reads a ton and critiques often. Her current plans include a Vespa and a road trip, despite eye-rolling objections from her adult children.

Books by Cassie Miles

HARLEQUIN INTRIGUE
832—ROCKY MOUNTAIN MANEUVERS*
874—WARRIOR SPIRIT
904—UNDERCOVER COLORADO**
910—MURDER ON THE MOUNTAIN**
948—FOOTPRINTS IN THE SNOW
978—PROTECTIVE CONFINEMENT†
984—COMPROMISED SECURITY†
999—NAVAJO ECHOES
1025—CHRISTMAS COVER-UP
1048—MYSTERIOUS MILLIONAIRE

*Colorado Crime Consultants
**Rocky Mountain Safe House
†Safe House: Mesa Verde

CAST OF CHARACTERS

Liz Norton—Working her way through law school, earning money as a part-time karate instructor and part-time private eye, she goes undercover as a maid.

Ben Crawford—His reputation as a millionaire adventurer masks his hard work, dedication to his family and his love for his five-year-old daughter, Natalie.

Jerod Crawford—The seventy-six-year-old patriarch of the wealthy, powerful family suffers from a brain tumor.

Charlene Crawford—Jerod's gold-digging trophy wife has a talent for ticking people off.

Patrice and Monte Welles—Ben's sister and her husband expect to inherit a fortune when her grandfather dies.

Al Mancini—As an almost-retired general practitioner, the doctor is out of his element in treating a brain tumor.

Tony Lansing—His drinking problem clouds his judgment as the Crawford family attorney.

Ramon Stephens—A male model, he knows everybody's secrets.

Victoria Crawford—Ben's estranged wife is suing for sole custody of their daughter.

Annette Peltier—Being a housemaid sparks her Cinderella dreams and fantasies.

Rachel Frakes—As housekeeper for the Crawford family, she demands perfection from her staff.

Harry Schooner—The former cop and owner of Schooner Detective Agency looks forward to retirement.

Chapter One

Being a part-time private eye put a serious crimp in Liz Norton's social life. At half-past eleven on a Friday night in May, she ought to be wearing lip gloss, dancing, flirting and licking the suds off a beer that somebody else had paid for. Instead, she'd spent the past two hours and seventeen minutes on stakeout with Harry Schooner, her sixty-something boss.

She slouched behind the steering wheel of Harry's beat-up Chevy. Even with the windows cracked for ventilation, she still smelled stale hamburger buns from the crumpled bags littering the backseat. On the plus side, the cruddy, old car blended with the rundown Denver neighborhood where they were parked at the curb away from the streetlight, watching and waiting.

In the passenger seat, Harry pressed his fist against his chest and grunted.

"Are you okay?" she asked.

"Heartburn."

His digestive system provided a source of constant complaint. Long ago, she'd given up lecturing him on the evils of a strictly fast-food diet. "Did you take your pill?"

"What are you? My mother?"

"A concerned employee," she said. "If you keel over from a heart attack, where am I going to find another job as glamorous as this one?"

He peeled off the silver wrapping on a roll of antacid tablets, popped the last one in his mouth and tossed the wrapper over his shoulder into the trashed-out backseat. "That reminds me. You're done with your semester. Right?"

"Took my last exam two days ago."

At age twenty-six, she'd put herself halfway through law school. The accomplishment made her proud, even though she still heard echoes of her mother's refrain: *"Why bother with an education? The only way a girl like you can make it is to find a man to support you."* This bit of advice came right before the grooming tips: *"Lighten your hair, shorten your skirts and stand up straight so your boobs stick out."*

Of course, Liz did the exact opposite. Her thick, multi-colored blond hair remained undyed and unstyled—except for her own occasional hacking to keep the jagged ends near chin-length. Her wardrobe included exactly one skirt—knee-length and khaki—that she'd picked up at a thrift store for a buck. Mostly, she wore jeans and T-shirts. Tonight, a faded brown one under a black windbreaker. As for Mom's advice to show off her chest, Liz had given up on that plan long ago. Even if she arched her back like a pretzel, nobody would ever confuse her with a beauty queen.

Her twice-married mom had actually done her a favor when she'd shoved her only daughter out the door on her eighteenth birthday and told her that she was on her own.

Liz had done okay. Without a man.

Harry groaned again and shifted in the passenger seat.

"You'll come to work for me full-time during your summer break. I could use the help. I'm getting too damn old for this job."

"Thanks, Harry." She'd been counting on this summer job. "But I still need Monday and Wednesday nights free to teach the under-twelve kids at the karate school."

"I got no problem with that." He made a wheezy noise through his nostrils and shrugged his heavy shoulders. His formerly athletic physique had settled into a doughy lump. Only his close-cropped white hair suggested the discipline of long-ago military service and twenty years as a cop. "How's my grandson doing at karate?"

"Not exactly a black belt, but he's hanging in there." She'd met Harry at Dragon Lou's Karate School when he'd come to watch his six-year-old grandson and ended up offering Liz a couple of part-time assignments.

Some aspects of being a P.I. were just plain nasty, like serving subpoenas or confirming the suspicions of a heartbroken wife about her cheating husband. But Liz enjoyed the occasional undercover disguise. Most of all, she liked grumpy old Harry and his two grown daughters. The Schooners represented the family she'd never had.

She peered through the scummy windshield at a ramshackle bungalow, landscaped with weeds and two rusty vehicles up on blocks. Gangsta music blared through the open windows. In the past hour, a half-dozen visitors had come and gone. She'd caught glimpses of three or four skinny children playing, even though it was way past normal bedtime, and she hoped the drug dealers inside the house weren't selling in front of the kids. Or to them.

"Are you sure we have the right address?"

"My source gave me the place, but not the time. He'll be here tonight." Harry rubbed his palms together. "Once we have photos of Mr. Crawford making a drug buy, we're in for a real big payday."

Liz found it hard to believe that Ben Crawford—millionaire adventurer and playboy—would show up in person. Didn't rich people hire underlings to do their dirty work?

But she hoped Harry was right. The Schooner Detective Agency could use the cash. They'd been retained by Ben's estranged wife, Victoria, who wanted enough dirt on her husband to void the prenup and gain sole custody of their five-year-old daughter. Photos of Ben making a drug buy would insure that Victoria got what she wanted, and she'd promised a huge bonus for the results.

Though Liz felt a twinge of regret about separating a father from his child, Ben Crawford deserved to be exposed. He'd been born with every advantage and was throwing his life away on drugs. In her book, that made him a lousy human being and definitely an unfit father.

A shiny, black Mustang glided to the curb in front of the house. This had to be their millionaire.

Harry shoved the camera into her hands. "You take the pictures. Don't worry. I'll back you up."

"Stay in the car, Harry."

"Get close to the front window," he said as he flipped open the glove compartment and took out an ancient Remington automatic.

A jolt of adrenaline turned her stakeout lethargy to tension. If Harry started waving his gun, this situation could get ugly. "Put that thing away."

"Don't you worry, Missy. I don't plan to shoot anybody." With another grunt, he opened his car door. "Go for the money shot. Crawford with the drugs in his hand."

The camera was foolproof—geared to automatically focus and adjust to minimal lighting. But she doubted she'd get a chance to use it. Most of the visitors to the house went inside, did their business and came out with hands shoved deeply into their pockets.

She darted across the street toward the dealer's house and ducked behind one of the junker cars in the driveway. Ben Crawford stood at the front door beside a bare bulb porch light. His shaggy brown hair fell over the collar of his worn denim shirt, only a few shades lighter than his jeans. He looked like a tall, rangy cowboy who had somehow gotten lost in the big city.

Holding the camera to her eye, Liz zoomed in on his face. *Wow.* Not only rich but incredibly good-looking, he had a firm jaw, high cheekbones and deep-set eyes. What was he doing here?

She pulled back on the zoom to include the dealer in his black mesh T-shirt and striped track pants. He pushed open the torn screen door and stepped onto the concrete slab porch under a rusted metal awning.

The pounding beat of rap music covered any noise Liz made as she clicked off several photos to make sure she caught them together.

Instead of going inside, Ben remained on the porch. For a moment, she hoped he wasn't here to make a buy, that there was a legitimate reason. Then he pulled a roll of bills from his pocket. The dealer handed over three brown, plastic vials.

Click. Click. Click. She had the money shot. A big payday for the Schooner Detective Agency.

The two men shook hands. Ben pivoted and returned to his Mustang while the dealer stood on the porch and watched Ben's taillights as he drove away.

Another man with a scraggly beard staggered outside and pointed.

Liz glanced over her shoulder to see what they were looking at. Harry crouched between two cars at the curb, his white hair gleaming in the moonlight.

"Hey, old man." The dealer came off the porch. "What the hell you doing?"

Harry straightened his stiff joints. "Guess I got lost."

"You watching us?" The two men stepped into the yard. From down the street, she heard ferocious barking, the prelude to a fight, and she knew Harry wasn't up to it.

She stashed the camera in the pocket of her windbreaker and rushed toward her partner. "There you are, Gramps. I've been looking all over for you." To the two men in the yard, she said, "Sorry if he bothered you. He wanders sometimes."

Their cold sneers told her that they weren't buying her story. The dealer snapped, "Stop right there, bitch."

"I'll just take Gramps home and—"

The crack of a gunshot brought her to a halt. She froze at the edge of the yard, praying that Harry wouldn't return fire. A shootout wouldn't be good for anybody.

Liz turned and faced the two men, who swaggered toward her. Her pulse raced, not so much from fear as uncertainty. She didn't know what to expect. Forcing an innocent smile, she said, "There's no need for guns."

"What's in your pocket? You carrying heat?"

As long as they didn't immobilize her, she ought to be able to take these two guys. Her five years studying martial arts at Dragon Lou's gave her an edge. Liz was capable of shattering a cinderblock with her bare hand.

From across the street, Harry yelled, "Leave her alone."

Please, Harry. Please don't use your gun. She had to act fast. No time to wait and see.

Liz aimed a flying kick at the bearded guy, neatly disarming him. Before his buddy could react, she whirled, chopped at his arm and kicked again. Though her hand missed, the heavy sole of her boot connected with his knee, and he stumbled.

The bearded man grabbed her forearm. Worst possible scenario. Both men had more brute strength than she did. Her advantage was speed and agility. She twisted and flipped, wrenching her arm free. He still clung to the sleeve of her windbreaker. She escaped by slipping out of her jacket.

Before they could brace themselves for another assault, she unleashed a series of kicks and straight-hand chops. Not a pretty, precise display. She wouldn't win any tournament points for style, but she got the job done with several swift blows to vulnerable parts of their anatomy. Throat. Gut. Groin.

Both were on their knees.

Another man rushed out the door. And another.

Behind her back, she heard Harry fire his automatic. Five shots.

She ran for the car.

Harry collapsed into the passenger side as she dived behind the wheel and cranked the ignition. Without turning on the headlights, she burned rubber and tore down the street.

Gunfire exploded behind them.

Liz didn't cut her speed until they reached a major intersection, where she turned on the headlights and merged into traffic. Her heart hammered inside her rib cage. They could have been killed. The aftermath of intense danger exploded behind her eyelids like belated fireworks.

Thank God for Dragon Lou and his martial arts training.

Beside her in the passenger seat, Harry was breathing heavily. With the back of his hand, he wiped sweat from his forehead. "Did you get the pictures?"

She cringed. "The camera was in my windbreaker. The bearded guy pulled it off me."

"It's okay."

"But you're not." She took note of his pasty complexion and heaving chest. "I'm taking you to the emergency room."

"You'd like that, wouldn't you? Kick the old man out of the way and take over his business."

"Yeah, that's my evil plan. Adding your debt to my student loans." Sarcasm covered her concern for him. "That's every girl's dream."

"Seriously, Liz. I don't need a doc." He exhaled in a long *whoosh* that dissolved into a hacking cough. "This was a little too much excitement for the old ticker."

"Is this your way of telling me that you have heart problems?"

"Forget it. Just drive back to the office."

Checking her rearview mirrors, she continued along Colfax Avenue. She didn't see anyone following them; they'd made a clean getaway. Just in case, she turned south at the next intersection and drove toward the highway. "We need to call the police."

"Nope."

"Harry, those guys shot at us. They assaulted us."

"But I returned fire." He cleared his throat, breathing more easily. His clenched fist lifted from his chest. "And you kicked ass. You might look like a Pop-Tart, but you were a fire-breathing dragon."

"My form wasn't terrific."

"You did good." He reached over and patted her shoulder. Always stingy with his compliments, Harry followed up with a complaint. "Too bad you messed up and lost the camera."

"Don't even think about taking the cost out of my wages." At a stoplight, she studied him again. He seemed to have recovered. "We need to fill out a police report. Those people are dealing drugs."

"And I guarantee that the narcs are well aware. Leave the drug dealers to the cops, we've got problems of our own. Like how to get that juicy bonus from Victoria."

Tomorrow, she'd put in a call to a friend at the Denver PD. At the very least, she wanted to see those children removed from a dangerous environment.

Harry sat up straighter. "Time to switch to Plan B."

"I don't like the sound of this."

"My source is the housekeeper who works at the Crawford estate near Evergreen. She can—"

"Wait a sec. How did you get to know a housekeeper?" She glanced toward the backseat. "You've never tidied up anything in your whole life."

"I served with her dad in Vietnam, and we stay in touch. Her name is Rachel Frakes. She's actually the one who recommended me to Victoria."

That connection explained a lot. The Schooner Detective Agency wasn't usually the first choice of the rich and famous. "What's Plan B?"

"Rachel gets you inside the estate. While you're there, you dig up the dirt on Ben."

"An undercover assignment."

That didn't sound too shabby. Maybe she'd impersonate a fancy-pants interior decorator. Or a horse wrangler. An upscale estate near Evergreen had to have several acres and a stable. Or she could be a guest—maybe an eccentric jet-setting heiress. A descendant of the Romanov czars. "Who am I supposed to be?"

He almost smiled. "You'll see."

Chapter Two

The next afternoon, Liz tromped down the back staircase from her brand-new undercover home—a third-floor garret at the Crawford mansion. Her starched gray uniform with the white apron reminded her of a Pilgrim costume she'd worn in fourth grade. The hem drooped below her knees, which was probably a good thing because she belatedly realized that she hadn't shaved her legs since before she started studying for final exams. Entering the kitchen, she adjusted the starched white cap that clung with four bobby pins to her unruly blond hair.

A maid. She was supposed to be a maid. The thrills just kept coming.

At the bottom of the staircase, Rachel the housekeeper stood with fists planted on her hips. She was a tall, solidly built woman who would have fit right in with the Russian women's weightlifting team. Her short blond hair was neatly slicked back away from her face. "Liz, may I remind you that a maid is supposed to be as unobtrusive as a piece of furniture."

"Okay." *Call me Chippendale.*

"While descending the staircase, you sounded like a herd of bison. We walk softly on the pads of our feet."

"If I walk softly, can I carry a big stick?"

Rachel's eyebrows shot up to her hairline. "Surely, you don't intend to hit anything."

"I'm joking." If this had been a real job, Liz would have already quit. "Any other advice?"

"The proper answer to a question is yes or no. Not 'okay.' And certainly not a joke. Is that clear?"

Liz poked at her silly white cap. "Yes, ma'am."

"Do something with your hair. It's all over the place."

She bit the inside of her mouth. "Yes, ma'am."

"No perfume. No nail polish. No makeup."

"No problem." That part of the assignment suited her normal procedure. "You know, Rachel, Harry and I really appreciate this—"

"Say nothing more." She pulled the door to the stairwell closed, making sure they were alone. "If anyone finds out what you're doing here, I'll deny any knowledge of your true profession."

"Yes, ma'am." In a low voice, she asked, "What can you tell me about Ben?"

"A fine-looking man but brooding. When Victoria told me about his drug problem, I had to act. I can't stand the thought of his daughter being raised by an addict."

"He doesn't usually live here, does he?"

"His home is in Seattle where he runs Crawford Aero-Equipment. They supply parts to the big airplane manufacturers and also build small custom jets."

Seemed like an extremely responsible job for a drug addict. "Why is he in Colorado?"

"This is his grandfather's house. Jerod Crawford." Her forehead pinched. "Jerod is a generous, brave man. He's dying from a brain tumor."

"And his grandson came home to take care of him."

Again, Ben's behavior wasn't what she'd expect from a druggie degenerate. Maybe he was here to make sure he inherited big bucks when grandpa died.

"For right now, you're needed in the kitchen," Rachel said. "We have a dinner party for sixteen scheduled for this evening."

Maybe some of these guests would provide negative evidence she could use against Ben. "Anybody I should watch for?"

"In what sense?"

"Other drug users. He must have gotten the name of his dealer from somebody."

"That's for you to investigate," Rachel said. "In the meantime, report to the kitchen."

"I'll be there in a flash. Right after I comb my hair."

Liz tiptoed up the stairs to the second floor. No matter what Rachel thought, her first order of business was to locate Ben's bedroom and search for his drug stash. She opened the door and stepped into the center of a long hallway decorated with oil paintings of landscapes hung above a natural cedar wainscoting. She peeked into an open door and saw an attractive bedroom with rustic furnishings—nothing opulent but a hundred times better than the tiny garret on the third floor where she'd dropped off her backpack and changed into the starchy maid outfit.

A tall brunette in a black pantsuit emerged from one of the rooms and stalked down the hallway.

Though Liz beamed a friendly smile, the brunette went past her without acknowledging her presence. Apparently, this was what it felt like to be furniture.

"Excuse me," Liz piped up.

The woman paused. "What?"

"I'm new here. And I'm looking for Ben's bedroom."

"My brother's room is right down there. Close to Grandpa."

The double doors to Jerod's room were open, and she heard other people inside. "Thank you."

There were too many people milling around to make a thorough search of Ben's room. Later, she'd come back. And right now? Liz wasn't anxious to report for maid duty in the kitchen. She'd use this time to explore, to get a sense of this sprawling house and the acreage that surrounded it.

On the drive here, she hadn't seen much. After the turnoff in Evergreen, she'd gone three-point-four miles on a narrow road that twisted through a thick forest of ponderosa pine, spruce and conifer. A wrought-iron gate between two stone pillars protected the entrance, and a chain-link fence enclosed the grounds. She'd had to identify herself over an intercom before the gates opened electronically.

The stone-and-cedar mansion nestled against a granite ridge. The main section rose three stories. Several different levels—landscaped terraces and cantilevered decks—made the house seem as though it had grown organically from the surrounding rocks and trees.

Liz went down a short hallway beside the staircase. A beveled glass door opened onto the second-story outdoor walkway made of wood planks. At the far end, the walkway opened onto a huge, sunlit deck.

Towering pines edged up to the railing. Hummingbird feeders and birdhouses hung from the branches. Several padded, redwood chairs and chaises faced outward to enjoy the view, but no one was outside. Floor-to-ceiling windows lined this side of the house, which was very likely Jerod Crawford's bedroom. Lucky for her, the drapes were closed.

As Liz walked to the railing, a fresh mountain breeze caressed her cheeks. Twitters from chipmunks and birds serenaded her. Multicolored petunias in attached wooden flower boxes bobbed cheerfully.

People like her didn't live in places like this. A grassy field dotted with scarlet Indian paintbrush and daisies rolled downhill, past a barn and another outbuilding, to a shimmering blue lake, surrounded by pines. In the distance, snow-covered peaks formed a majestic skyline.

At the edge of the lake, a wood dock stretched into the water. Though she was over a hundred yards away, she thought she recognized Ben. He faced a woman with platinum-blond hair and a bright red sweater.

Though Liz couldn't hear their words, they were obviously arguing. The woman gestured angrily. Ben pulled back as though he couldn't stand being close to her.

She stamped her foot.

And then, she slapped him.

BEN RESTRAINED AN URGE to strike back at Charlene. Much as she had earned the right to have her ass thrown off his grandpa's property, that wasn't Ben's call.

Through tight lips, he said, "You're not always going to have things your way."

"No matter what you think, I'm the one in charge around here. Me. I'm Jerod's wife."

A ridiculous but undeniably true statement. At age thirty-six, she was only two years older than Ben himself. He hated having to consult with her on his grandpa's medical care and would never understand why the old man listened to her.

"Be reasonable, Charlene. I've been talking to specialists and neurosurgeons. They think Jerod's tumor could be removed."

"I don't want your doctors." She screeched like a harpy. "Jerod is happy with Dr. Mancini. And so am I."

Dr. Al Mancini had been the Crawford family doctor for years, and he was competent to treat sniffles and scraped knees. But a brain tumor? "Mancini isn't even practicing anymore. He's retired."

"And Jerod is his only patient. Dr. Mancini comes here every single day. Your specialist would put Jerod in the hospital. And he refuses."

Unfortunately, Charlene was correct. His stubborn, Texas-born grandpa had planted himself here and wouldn't budge. Every day, the tumor inside his head continued to grow. His vision was seriously impaired, and he barely had the strength to get out of his wheelchair. "If not an operation, he needs access to other treatments. Radiation. Cutting-edge medications."

"He won't go. And I'm not going to force him."

For the moment, he abandoned this topic. There were other bones to pick. "At least, cancel your damn dinner party. Jerod needs peace and quiet."

"You want to pretend like he's already dead. Well, he's not. He needs activity and excitement. That's why he married me."

"Really? I thought it had more to do with your thirty-six double-D chest."

She slapped him again. This time, he'd earned it.

With a swish of her hips, Charlene flounced up the hill toward the house.

Five years ago, when his grandpa had announced that he wanted to marry a Las Vegas showgirl, Ben had been almost proud of the old guy. After a lifetime of hard work that had started in the Texas oil fields, Jerod had the right to amuse himself. Even if it meant the rest of the family had to put up with a gold digger.

Charlene had readily agreed to a very generous prenuptial agreement. Whether their marriage was ended by divorce or death, she walked away with a cool half million in cash. Not a bad deal.

Ben had expected Charlene to divorce his grandpa after a year and grab the cash, but she'd stayed...and stayed...and stayed. In her shallow way, she might even love Jerod. And he had to admit that their May–December marriage had turned out better than his. Nothing good had come from that union, except for his daughter.

He walked to the end of the small dock. A spring wind rippled the waters. Trout were jumping. In the rolling foothills of Colorado, he saw the swells of the ocean. He missed his home in Seattle that overlooked the sea, but he cherished every moment here with his grandpa as the old man prepared for his final voyage.

Behind his back, Ben heard someone step onto the dock. Had Charlene come back? He turned and saw a gray maid's uniform. "What is it?"

"You must be Ben." She marched toward him with her hand outthrust. "I'm Liz Norton. The new maid."

He accepted her handshake. Though she was a slender little thing, her grip was strong. He took a second look at her. The expression in her luminous green eyes showed a surprising challenge. Not the usual demeanor for household staff. "Is this your first job as a servant?"

"Servant?" Her nose wrinkled in disgust. "I can't say that I like that job description. Sounds like I ought to curtsey."

"I suppose you have a more politically correct job title in mind."

She pulled her hand away from his grasp and thought for half a second. "Housekeeping engineer."

In spite of her droopy gray uniform, she radiated electricity, which might explain why her hair looked like she'd stuck her finger in a wall socket. He would have dismissed her as being too cute. Except for the sharp intelligence in her green eyes.

"Nice place you've got here." She stepped up beside him. "Are there horses?"

"Not anymore. Horses were my grandmother's passion. Arabians. God, they were beautiful." He had fond memories of grooming the horses with his grandmother. "After she passed away, ten years ago, Jerod sold them to someone who would love them as much as she had."

"Wise decision. Every living creature needs to be with someone who loves them."

A hell of a profound statement. "Are you? With someone who loves you?"

"I do okay." She cocked her head and looked up at him. "How about you, Ben? Who loves you?"

"My daughter," he responded quickly. "Natalie."

Her expression went blank as if she had something to hide. All of a sudden, her adorable freckled face seemed less innocent. He wondered why she'd approached him, why she spoke of love.

There had been incidents in the past when female employees had tried to seduce him, but Liz's body language wasn't flirtatious. Her arms hung loosely at her sides. Her feet were planted solidly. Something else motivated her.

"You have a reputation as an adventurer," she said.

"What kind of stuff do you do? Something with the airplanes you manufacture?"

"I test-pilot our planes. Not for adventure. It's work."

She arched an eyebrow. "Cool job."

"I'm not complaining." He glanced up the hill toward the house. It was time to get his grandpa outside in the sun. Maybe he could talk some sense into the old man. "Please excuse me, Liz."

Instead of stepping politely aside, she stayed beside him, matching her gait to his stride. "I think I met your sister at the house. Real slim. Dressed in black."

"That's Patrice." And *not* good news. He'd known that his sister and her husband, Monte, were coming to dinner, but he hadn't expected her until later. As a rule, he tried to keep his sister and Charlene separate. The two women hated each other.

"Is your sister married?" Liz asked.

"Yes."

"Any kids?"

Patrice was far too selfish to spoil her rail-thin figure by getting pregnant. "None."

From the house, he heard a high-pitched scream.

Ben took off running.

When he looked over, he saw Liz with her uniform hiked up, racing along beside him. She had to be the most unusual maid he'd ever met.

Chapter Three

Liz charged up the incline from the lake toward the house. Though her legs churned at top speed, she couldn't keep pace with Ben's stride.

She heard a second scream...and a third that trailed off into an incoherent, staccato wail that reminded her of a kid throwing a tantrum in the grocery store aisle. The cries seemed to be coming from the front entrance.

Trailing behind Ben, she couldn't help but admire his running form. His long legs pumped. His forest-green shirt stretched tightly across his muscular shoulders. For a supposed drug addict, he appeared to be in amazing physical condition. As he approached the shiny, black Escalade parked at the front door, he muttered, "Son of a bitch."

Two bitches, actually. Beside the SUV, two women grappled. Patrice shrieked again. Still clad in her sleek black pantsuit, she had both arms clutched possessively around a large metal object. Charlene tugged at her arms and delivered a couple of ineffectual swats on Patrice's skinny bottom.

Liz stopped and stared at the spectacle of two grown women scuffling like brats on a playground. She didn't envy Ben as he waded into the middle of the wrestling match and pulled them apart. "What the hell is going on?"

Without loosening her grip on what appeared to be a two-foot-tall bronze statue of a rearing bronco, Patrice tossed her head. Her smooth, chin-length mahogany hair fell magically into place. "Grandma Crawford gave this original Remington to me. It once belonged to Zane Grey, you know."

"You're a thief." Charlene jabbed in her direction with a red manicured fingernail that matched her sweater. "How dare you come to *my house* and steal from me."

"*Your* house?"

"That's right." Charlene's blue eyes flashed like butane flames. "I'm Jerod's wife. All this is mine."

Patrice's nostrils flared as she inhaled and exhaled loudly. She spat her words. "You. Are. Sadly. Mistaken."

"I'll show you who's wrong." Charlene lunged.

Ben caught the small woman by her waist, lifted her off her feet, carried her a few paces and dropped her. "Stop it," he growled. "Both of you."

Other residents of the house had responded to the shrieks. The gardener and chauffeur peeked around a hedge. On the landing, a man in a chef hat hovered behind another maid with eyes round as silver dollars. Rachel Frakes glared disapprovingly. When her gaze hit Liz, she remembered the lecture on decorum and reached up to adjust the starched white maid's cap that hung precariously from one bobby pin.

Ben strode toward his sister. "Give me the damn horse."

"It's mine." She stuck out her chin. "Besides, you're supposed to be on *my* side."

"Give it to me. Now." His eyes—which were an incredible shade of teal—narrowed. An aura of command and determination emanated from him, and Liz recognized the strong charisma of a born leader. It would take a stronger woman than Patrice to stand up to Ben.

His right hand closed around the neck of the rearing bronco, and he gave a tug. Reluctantly, his sister released her grip.

Quickly, he passed the sculpture to Liz. "Would you take this inside, please."

"Sure." She remembered her earlier conversation with Rachel about proper responses and amended, "I mean, yes."

The burnished bronze was still warm from being cradled against Patrice's body. Liz held it gingerly. She wasn't a big fan of Western art, even if it had belonged to the legendary Western writer Zane Grey, but this lump of metal must be worth a lot.

Ben turned back to Patrice and Charlene. "Shake hands and make up, ladies."

"No way," Charlene responded. "I'm not going to touch that skinny witch."

"This feud has gone far enough." His baritone took on an ominous rumble. "Like it or not, we're family. We stick together."

Liz edged around the three of them on her way toward the front door. This squabble—though plenty juicy and perversely entertaining—really wasn't her concern. Her job as a private investigator meant finding evidence proving that Ben was an unfit father—a task that had taken on a layer of complication. She'd expected him to be an addict or a crazed playboy or an irresponsible adventurer. None of those identities fit. He seemed family oriented and rational…even admirable.

Before Liz could step inside, a well-tanned man—dressed in the male version of Patrice's black suit—appeared in the doorway and struck a pose as if waiting for a *GQ* photographer. Though his blond hair was thinning on top, he'd compensated with a long ponytail. He squinted at Liz's face, then his gaze caught on the sculpture. "What do you think you're doing with that horse?"

"I was planning to saddle up and ride in the Kentucky Derby."

"It's mine." He gestured toward Patrice. "Ours."

"And who are you?" Liz inquired. "The great-grandson of Zane Grey? A Rider of the Purple Sage?"

"Monte. Monte Welles." *Like Bond. James Bond.* "Patrice's husband."

When he made the mistake of reaching for the statue that had been entrusted to her care by Ben, her reaction came from pure instinct. With both arms busy holding the bronze horse, Liz relied on her feet. Two quick, light kicks tapped on his ankle, then the toe of his left foot.

He gave a yelp and backed off. "You're fired."

"The hell she is," Ben said. "Monte, get your butt over here and talk some sense into your wife. She and Charlene need to kiss and make up."

"Hah!" Patrice tossed her head again. "I'd rather kiss a toad."

"I'll bet," Charlene countered. "That's why you married Monte."

Liz stifled a chuckle. Though she wasn't taking sides, she gave a point to Charlene for her nifty insult.

Patrice planted her fists on her nonexistent hips. "Leave my husband out of this."

"Gladly."

"And I want an apology. I wasn't stealing. Just reclaiming something that belongs to me."

"Wrong," Charlene said. "This is my house. Everything in it belongs to me."

"Not for long—prenup. Remember the prenup," Patrice said smugly. "When Jerod dies, you get a payoff and nothing more. Not a stick of furniture. Not one square foot of property. And certainly not my Remington sculpture."

A sly grin curved Charlene's glossy lips. "What would you say if I told you that Jerod has decided to change his will?"

Patrice looked like she might faint. Her complexion went ghostly pale. Her arms fell limply to her sides. "How could you say such a thing?"

"Maybe because it's true." Charlene preened. "You can check with the family attorney. He'll be at dinner."

"Grandpa wouldn't do that," she mumbled. "He couldn't. Not on his deathbed."

"He's not going to die," Charlene said with vehement conviction. "He's going to get better."

"Damn straight, honey. You tell 'em."

Those few words, spoken in a Texan drawl, riveted everyone's attention to the doorway. A white-haired man in a wheelchair was pushed onto the landing by a nurse in scrubs. Dark sunglasses perched on his beaklike nose. A plaid wool bathrobe hung from the frame of his shoulders. Though debilitated by illness, he was clearly the patriarch. Jerod Crawford, age seventy-six, took immediate, unquestioned control of the situation. "You girls quit your squabbling. And I mean now."

A laugh bubbled from Charlene's lips as she bounced toward her husband, leaned down and planted a quick kiss on his forehead. "You look good today. Excited about our party?"

"I'm waiting to see what you'll wear. I like you all gussied up and smelling like roses."

"I know you do." She checked her wristwatch. "I need to run into town and pick up my dress from the seamstress. Don't get yourself too tired before our guests arrive."

"Ain't much strain sitting in this here chair."

She held both of his gnarled hands and squeezed. "Take care, lover boy. You're my bumblebee."

"And you're my honey."

Even though Charlene was probably a gold digger, Liz thought her fondness for Jerod rang true. Likewise for Ben, who stepped behind his grandpa's wheelchair and pushed him along the driveway toward a narrow asphalt path leading toward the lake.

Rachel tapped Liz's shoulder. "Put the sculpture on the table in the den and report to the kitchen."

"Yes, ma'am."

As she entered the house, Liz reflected. She'd learned a lot about the dynamics of the Crawford family. Their greed. Their hostility. The seething undercurrent of hate and anger masked by these luxurious surroundings. Unfortunately, she'd gained zero evidence that Ben was an unfit father.

LIZ ALWAYS HAD TROUBLE following orders, but she tried to do as Rachel asked. Now she was baffled. Her assignment was to put together the place settings with half a dozen utensils, four plates, three different glasses and cup and saucer. She stood at the head of the table, shuffled the forks, switched the positions of the wineglass and water glass. Was that how it went?

When she looked up and saw Ben watching her with an amused smile, she felt a hot flush creeping up her throat. Blushing? She hadn't blushed since sophomore year of high school when the captain of the baseball team had kissed her in the hallway, and she'd let him get to second base.

Ben came closer. "Could you use some help?"

Embarrassed about blushing, she thought of icebergs and snowstorms—anything to cool her off. Though she hated to admit that she didn't have a clue about the third fork, Liz feared that Rachel would have a coronary if the place settings weren't perfect. "I could use some expert advice."

His shoulder brushed her arm as he reached across the plate setting to rearrange the knives. She was aware of his bodily warmth and a natural masculine scent that was far more enticing than aftershave. Not that she should be noticing the way he smelled. Her focus should be on gathering evidence to prove that he was an unfit father.

When he finished with the formal setting and stepped back, she nodded. "I knew that."

He gave her a sidelong glance. "Did you?"

"Not really, but it's not something that bothers me. In the grand scheme of things, why should I waste brain cells on knowing where to put the forks?"

"You're not really a maid. Sorry, housekeeping engineer. Why are you really here?"

His intense blue-eyed gaze rested suspiciously upon

her face. He wanted the truth, which wasn't something she could give.

From her other undercover experiences, she'd learned that successful lies were based on truth, so she stuck to reality. "I'm a law student, paying my own way. I need a summer job, and I heard about this maid gig through a friend of a friend."

His scrutiny continued; he wasn't totally satisfied with her answer. "I liked the way you handled Monte. You know karate."

Now the truth got more complicated. If she mentioned Dragon Lou, Ben might check her out with a phone call, which might lead to someone mentioning her part-time work as a private eye. "I learned the basics of self-defense. Seemed like a smart thing for a woman living alone."

Having offered a rational explanation, she should have stopped talking but really wanted him to believe her. She continued, "You probably won't find it hard to believe that I've gotten myself into a few scrapes. About six years ago, I went out with this guy…" A warning voice inside her head told her to shut up. *Shut up, now.* "Maybe I had too much to drink. Maybe he did. I don't know."

Ben's attention never wavered. "Go on."

"Somehow," she said, "I ended up at his apartment. He got aggressive. When I told him no, he didn't stop."

She had never told anyone—not her mother, not her friends, not Harry Schooner—about that night. She'd been date raped. Remembering her weakness made her sad and angry at the same time. "That's when I started taking karate lessons. And I'm good. No one can force me to do something I don't want to do. Never again. No means no."

He took a step toward her, and she feared he would offer sympathy. A shoulder to cry on. Or a gentle platitude that could never make things better.

Instead he shook her hand. "Smart decision, Liz."

"Thank you, Ben."

She was beginning to really like this guy.

Chapter Four

To Liz, the flurry of anticipation and activity surrounding the arrival of the dinner guests seemed out of proportion. It wasn't as if the Queen of England would be popping by for a state dinner. Her attitude was in direct contrast to the other maid, Annette Peltier, who twittered excitedly as she rearranged the centerpiece on the dining room table.

"Isn't it beautiful?" Annette gushed. Her maid's cap nestled perfectly above a neat chignon at the back of her head. "I just love these dinner parties."

"Who's coming, anyway?"

"Patrice and her husband. He's a famous athlete, you know."

"Monte? What sport?"

"He was in the winter Olympics. In the biathalon. The one where they ski and shoot. He's a marksman."

"Who else?"

"Dr. Mancini and Tony Lansing, the family lawyer." She fussed over the elegant china and crystal, adjusting the place settings one centimeter left, then right. "And Charlene's friends from Denver. They're so beautiful, especially Ramon Stephens. He's dreamy."

Rachel came into the dining room and gave a snort. "Watch out for Ramon when he has a couple of martinis in him. That young man thinks he's God's gift to women."

Though there were wineglasses on the table, Liz hadn't noticed a liquor setup. "Where's the bar?"

"In the downstairs lounge. Which is, undoubtedly, where they'll go after dinner."

"I used to be a bartender. Maybe I could—"

"Why didn't you mention this before?" For the first time, Rachel regarded her as though she were more than a waste of space. "Bartending will be your primary assignment. Run downstairs and make sure everything is in order."

"I'm on it."

"Liz, please," Rachel chided. "Proper response."

"Yes, ma'am."

Liz skipped down the staircase into a long, low room with a beamed ceiling and a fireplace. Classic leather furniture arrayed around a red-felt pool table and giant flat-screen television. The carved cherrywood bar was stocked with an inventory of mixes for a very upscale selection of liquor. Nothing but the best for the Crawfords.

In the fridge, Liz found garnishes—lemons, limes, cherries and olives—everything she'd need for cocktails. An impressive bit of organization.

From upstairs, she heard the chatter of the first guests arriving. She ought to trot up there and see if she could be helpful, but Liz wasn't planning on winning any prizes for Maid of the Year. Instead, she went to the far end of the room where sliding glass doors opened onto the forest. Outside, the sun dipped toward the mountains and colored the underbellies of clouds with a golden glow. From this vantage point, she could see down to the lake.

To the south, there were two outbuildings. The big one was probably where the Arabian stallions of the first Mrs. Jerod Crawford had been kept. The other, constructed of rough logs, had only one story with garage-sized double doors across the front.

As she watched, she saw Ben emerge from a side door of the log barn. Though she was too far away to clearly see what he was doing, it looked like he was fastening a lock on the door. That kind of secrecy suggested nefarious purposes. The barn might be where he hid his drug stash.

How could he be an addict? The guy reeked of integrity. But she'd seen him making a buy from the dealer in Denver. Seen him with her own eyes.

She went back into the lounge in time to greet two men coming down the stairs. The white-haired man, neatly packaged in a three-piece gray suit with a red bow tie, was Dr. Al Mancini, the family doctor, who had been pointed out to her when he'd arrived at the house. Though the other man wore a casual sweater and jeans, he had the arrogance of a well-paid professional. From his precisely trimmed brown hair to his buffed fingernails, he was polished. In law school, she'd learned to recognize these guys on sight: lawyers. This had to be Tony Lansing, family attorney.

"Gentlemen," she said. "May I get you something to drink?"

Barely noticing her, the doc ordered a whiskey on the rocks. The attorney wanted vodka with a twist.

"About Jerod's new will," the doctor said.

"I can't discuss it, except to say that the amended document has just been signed, witnessed and filed away in my briefcase."

"I can guess what it says." The doctor leaned his elbow on the bar with the attitude of someone accustomed to drinking. In spite of his white hair, he didn't look all that ancient. He was probably only in his fifties. "Jerod intends to cut the family and leave the bulk of his estate to Charlene. Is that about right, Tony?"

"I can't say."

But he gave a nearly imperceptible nod. Liz hadn't come to the Crawford estate to investigate family matters, but the intrigue surrounding Jerod's will was too juicy to ignore. She placed the whiskey on the bar in front of the doctor. With a deft flick of a paring knife, she peeled off a lemon twist for the vodka.

Picking up his whiskey, the doctor said, "I've known Jerod for nearly twenty years. He's no fool. Charlene hasn't tricked him into leaving her the millions. I think he truly loves that little blond cupcake."

"Can't blame him for that."

"But here's the kicker. I think she loves him back. If Charlene wasn't here to enforce what Jerod wants, Ben would have put the old man in a hospital with a troop of specialists poking and prodding."

Which didn't sound like such a bad idea to Liz. Jerod had a brain tumor and gazillions of bucks to spend on medical treatment. Why not get the very best care?

Both men drank in silence.

The doctor licked his lips and grinned. "There's one big problem with the new will."

"What's that?" Tony asked.

"Patrice is going to kill Charlene."

When the two men had finished their drinks, Liz cleaned up the glasses. Straightening the starched white maid cap on her unruly blond hair, she ascended the staircase into a maelstrom of activity. Guests had been greeted at the door with flutes of champagne and were mostly in the living room, where a wall of windows displayed a magenta sunset. Patrice wore her trademark black, but the other women were a couture rainbow. The men were equally chic but in more subdued tones.

Her gaze went immediately to Ben. Though he still wore jeans, he'd thrown on a white fisherman's knit sweater that made his shoulders look impossibly broad. She was surprised to find him looking back at her. With a subtle grin and a lift of his eyebrow, he communicated volumes. He'd been here before, heard all the chitchat before. And he'd rather be standing by the lake counting the ripples. Or soaring through the sunset in a sleek jet.

Or maybe she was reading too much into a glance.

Purposely turning away, Liz reported to the kitchen, where she did her best to follow the orders of the very nervous chef and Rachel.

Throughout the dinner, her assigned task would be serving each course and unobtrusively whisking away the dirty dishes. Her *real* agenda? Listening for clues. One of these guests might be Ben's drug connection. He took a seat at the foot of the table. To his right sat an impassive blond woman with a plunging neckline and arms as skinny as pipe cleaners. Though she was as gaunt as a heroin addict, Liz guessed that her vacant expression came from hunger rather than drugs. On Ben's left was Tony Lansing, who held up his empty cocktail glass, signaling to Liz that he wanted a refill.

She darted downstairs, whipped up another vodka with a twist and returned to the dining room in time to see Jerod make his entrance. Rising from his wheelchair, he leaned on Charlene's arm as he made his way to the head of the table.

Illness had not diminished the charisma of this former Texas oil baron's personality. As he greeted his guests, he showed dignity rather than weakness. Nor did Charlene treat him like an invalid. Standing close at his side, she effortlessly outshone every other woman in the room. Though small and slim, her hot-pink dress emphasized her curves. Her blond hair caught the light from the chandelier and shimmered as she gave her husband a peck on the cheek and took a seat beside him.

"I'm hungry as a bear," Jerod announced. "Let's eat."

Liz and the rest of the staff leaped into action. Serving a formal dinner wasn't as simple as when she'd worked as a waitress in a pancake house. Though she tried to follow the moves of Annette and Rachel, she bumped against chairs and the shoulders of the guests. The appetizer plates made loud clinks when she placed them into the formal setting. When she cleared those plates and stacked them one on top of the other, Rachel was waiting for her in the kitchen.

"You're doing it all wrong," she snapped. "Take the plates two at a time. One in each hand and return them to the kitchen."

"Seems like a waste of time," Liz said.

"This china is antique and worth a small fortune. Handle it carefully. We don't want chips."

Serving the clear consommé soup was a choreographed ritual with Liz holding the tureen while Annette ladled. Should have been easy. But Liz had never before moved with a glide. Her steps bounced. The soup sloshed. Hot droplets hit her hands, clinging tightly to the handles.

Don't drop it. Whatever you do, don't drop this slippery, heavy piece of heirloom china.

When they got to Ben, he looked up at her. "Are we having fun yet?"

How would you like this whole tureen dumped onto your lap, Mister? She muttered, "Yes, sir."

When the main course—filet mignon so tender that it could be cut with a fork—hit the table, Liz realized that she hadn't eaten. Hunger pangs roiled in her belly as she stood at attention with a pitcher of ice water to replenish the glasses. She tensed her abs. *Don't growl. Please, stomach. Don't growl.*

Dinner conversation twittered around the table. Though the basic topics involved golf scores and vacation plans for the summer, Liz recognized an undercurrent of tension in the too-shrill laughter and hostile grimaces. Patrice fired hate-filled stares at Charlene. One of the couples were former lovers who sniped mercilessly at each other. The dark, handsome man who sat to Charlene's left eyeballed her cleavage with undisguised longing and spewed compliments as if Charlene herself had cooked this fabulous dinner. That had to be the infamous Ramon.

As she leaned close to Ben to fill his water glass, her stomach let loose with a roar loud enough to stop conversation at that end of the table.

Patrice glared at her.

Rachel gaped.

Gallantly, Ben patted his own belly. "Excuse me," he said. "I must be enjoying the meal."

Instead of being grateful, Liz felt a surge of annoyance. She didn't need for him to rescue her from embarrassment; she had nothing to be ashamed of. But her cheeks burned. Another blush?

At that moment, she hated all these people with their expensive clothes, hidden agendas and cost-a-fortune dishes. She remembered every time she'd been hungry—not from a self-imposed diet but because she couldn't afford a loaf of bread. In the real world, stomachs growled, and she wanted to stand up and take credit. Demure, silent serving definitely wasn't her thing.

Tony Lansing waggled his cocktail glass at her. "I'd like another."

"Yes, sir."

Though he was the only person drinking hard liquor, the others had gone through more than a dozen bottles of wine. The pipe-cleaner woman next to Ben had barely touched her food but managed to polish off several glasses of Chablis. She leaned to the left like the Tower of Pisa.

Downstairs at the bar, Liz attacked the garnishes in the fridge, devouring a blood orange in two seconds flat. Of course, she drooled the juice onto the front of her uniform. *Of course.*

Her choices were to go through the rest of the meal with a big, fat stain on her chest or to wash it out and be soggy. Another idea popped into her head. She could go up to her maid's garret bedroom and change—maybe using the time to make a quick search in Ben's bedroom.

After she delivered the vodka to Tony Lansing, she pointed out the stain to Rachel. "I should change."

"No time," she said. "Clear the dinner plates. Serve the dessert. Then you can change."

She whipped through her duties, noting that a couple

of guests had already left the table to take bathroom breaks or "freshen up."

As soon as the last dessert plate was delivered, she headed for the back staircase, ducking into a darkened hallway off the kitchen. There was just enough light for her to see a couple locked in a passionate kiss.

Consumed by desire, they didn't notice her. But Liz soaked in every detail. The bouncy blond hair belonged to Charlene. The man was the very polished lawyer, Tony Lansing. Their embrace put a whole different light on Jerod's changed will. They might be working together to siphon all the money away from the Crawford estate. Should she tell Ben? Was it any of her business?

The overhead hallway light flashed on. Ramon charged past her.

"Bastard," he shouted as he stalked toward the couple.

Charlene and Tony broke apart. In the sudden burst of light, she blinked wildly. Her bruised lips parted in a breathless gasp. Tony seemed disoriented, which wasn't a surprise to Liz. The lawyer had tossed back a gallon of wine and three vodkas during dinner.

Ramon's arm raised over his head.

Liz saw the glint of light on a kitchen knife. Her reaction was pure reflex. She kicked hard at the back of Ramon's knee, sending him sprawling against the wall.

He whirled, facing her. "Stay out of this," he warned.

"Drop your weapon."

He lowered the blade, threatening her.

There wasn't much room to maneuver in the narrow corridor, and the skirt on her uniform restricted her ability to kick high. Aiming carefully, she delivered a quick chop to his wrist. The knife clattered to the floor.

Ramon blocked her next blow. He flung his entire

body at her, pinning her to the wall. His breath smelled like the inside of a garbage disposal. "Not so tough now, are you?"

The only way out of this hold was a knee to the groin as soon as he gave her the space to strike. And she was looking forward to that ultimately disabling attack.

Before she could act, Ramon was yanked away from her and thrown facedown on the floor.

Ben stood over his prone body with the heel of his boot planted firmly between Ramon's shoulder blades. He turned toward Liz. "Are you all right?"

"I could have taken him down," she said as she adjusted her stained uniform. "I don't need you to rescue me."

"I'll keep that in mind." He looked down at the knife on the floor, then confronted Tony and Charlene. "I want an explanation."

"A misunderstanding," Tony said smoothly. "Nothing to worry about."

"He lies," Ramon wailed from the floor. "He has insulted me. And my beautiful Charlene."

Ben lifted him off the floor as if the muscular young man weighed no more than a sack of feathers. Ben's large hand clamped around Ramon's throat.

"Charlene is Jerod's wife," Ben reminded him. "She doesn't belong to you."

Charlene rushed forward. "Let him go, Ben."

"I want this son of a bitch out of here."

"Too damned bad." Charlene tossed her head. "This is my house. I say who stays and who goes. Ramon amuses me."

A vein in Ben's forehead throbbed, and Liz sympathized with his anger. Some women enjoyed having men fight over them; the danger acted as an aphrodisiac. Indeed, Charlene appeared to be turned on. Her lips drew back from her whitened teeth. "I want Ramon to stay. And Tony, too."

The lawyer found his voice. "Actually, I should be going. Thought I could catch a ride with Doctor Al."

"If you must," Charlene said.

"Thank you," he said in a formal tone that was comical, given the threatening situation. "For a lovely evening."

When the lawyer sidled out of the hallway, Ben released his hold on Ramon who slouched forward, rubbing his throat.

"One more thing," Ben said to him. "Apologize to the lady."

Ramon turned toward Charlene. "You know I would never hurt you. From the bottom of my heart, I am—"

"Not her," Ben interrupted by physically turning him toward Liz. "Apologize to this lady."

Ramon's dark eyebrows pulled down in an angry scowl. His full lips pursed as he forced the words. "I am sorry."

"Accepted," Liz said quickly. She definitely wanted this episode to be over.

"There," Charlene said. "Everything's fine. And the night is young. I want to have some real fun tonight."

In a low, dangerous voice, Ben warned, "Be careful what you ask for, Charlene."

Chapter Five

Less than an hour later, Ben accompanied his grandpa upstairs to his bedroom suite, where the nurse would help him into bed.

"Wish I could stay awake," Jerod said. "Charlene's friends remind me of the days when I used to party all night long. Then I'd go home with the prettiest little gal in the whole damn place."

"Good times," Ben muttered with thinly disguised insincerity. He'd never been as social as his grandpa.

"Listen up, boy. It's high time you find yourself a girlfriend."

"Technically, I'm still married to Victoria." They'd been living apart for over a year—far apart. Victoria had taken up residence in the Denver house while Ben stayed in Seattle, where his business was based.

The final court date for their divorce was in a couple of weeks, and he'd gotten to the point where he would gladly relinquish all the cash and property she wanted. But not custody. He'd never give up one precious moment with his beautiful five-year-old daughter. Natalie was the one bright spot in his life.

"Ain't telling you to get married," Jerod said. "But it

wouldn't hurt to start dating. Weren't you sitting next to some cute thing at dinner?"

"Not my type."

The only woman at dinner who had appealed to him was Liz. When he'd stepped into that hallway and had seen Ramon crushing her against the wall, he'd wanted to kill that sleazy jerk for laying his hands on her. If she'd given the word, he would have happily dragged Ramon out the door and thrown him in the lake. But those weren't Liz's wishes. Instead of fawning, she'd coolly informed him that she could take care of herself.

He had no doubt that she could have handled the situation. If he hadn't intruded, she probably would have broken both Ramon's kneecaps and knocked out his front teeth. He grinned at his mental image of a karate queen with tangled hair and a prickly attitude. Definitely a woman who could kick ass.

"What you need," his grandpa said, "is to get back on the horse. Sure, you got bucked off once. That don't mean it's time to hang up your spurs."

"We're still talking about women, right?"

"Women. Horses. Same basic rules apply."

Ben chuckled. If he compared Liz to the old gray mare, she'd likely buck him through a plate-glass window. "Sleep well, Grandpa."

The hallway on the upper floor was calm and quiet. This multi-level house had been well built and sound-proofed with plenty of room for noisy family or guests. Ben was tempted to retire to his bedroom and forget about the party that was ongoing in the lounge, but Charlene and her friends were as irresponsible as two-year-olds. He needed to keep an eye on things. To quell fights if they got physical and make sure nobody ripped off their clothes and dived into the lake. For the rest of the night, Ben would be the self-appointed sheriff.

He descended to the main floor, where Rachel and the staff bustled around, cleaning up the dining room and kitchen. He paused to compliment her and the chef on a job well done.

Then he went downstairs into the noise. With the fully stocked bar, carefully placed lighting and a state-of-the-art sound system, the lounge easily duplicated the atmosphere of a small, private club for eight or nine of Charlene's friends. He wasn't sure how many, couldn't be bothered to remember their names. The guys seemed to be varying shades of Ramon. Big talkers. Some with trust funds. One of them—Andy?—Arty?—wanted to sell him a used Mercedes. As for the women—these were high-maintenance babes—much like his estranged wife. Been there, done them.

He was glad to see Liz stationed behind the bar. She'd discarded her maid cap and rolled up the sleeves on her uniform. For an apron, she wore a black sweatshirt with the arms tied tightly around her tiny waist. It was a goofy outfit that she somehow made look sexy as she juggled a silver martini shaker, poured a drink and garnished it with two olives speared on a toothpick. She slid the glass across the bar to a young man with a shaved head, who sipped, gave her an approving nod and strolled back to the pool table.

Ben rested an elbow on the bar. "You've done this before."

"I'm a lot better at mixing drinks than serving a formal dinner."

"You did fine."

"Tell that to my growling belly. So, what'll you have?"

Her nose crinkled when she grinned. "No, wait. Let me guess."

"Another of your hidden talents? You're psychic?"

"No, but I'm a pretty decent bartender. That means remembering what people drink."

He gestured to the guy who was walking away. "How will you remember him?"

"Baldy likes olives. That's easy." She lowered her voice to a conspiratorial level. "See the woman with black hair and a hateful attitude? She's a Bloody Mary."

And a potential problem. Bloody Mary looked like she might go ballistic. "What about Charlene?"

"Top-of-the-line champagne. Lots of fizz and bubbles. And I wouldn't try to pull a substitute because she'd know the difference."

"How about Ramon?"

"Vodka and orange juice, the typical screwdriver. But with 7-UP. I call it a screwup."

"Appropriate," he said. "If I hadn't shown up when I did, what would have been your next move?"

"Groin." She illustrated with an emphatic jab of her knee.

He winced in sympathetic pain. "I'm glad you're here. If things start getting out of hand—"

"I've got your back." Her green eyes studied him. "Now, let me figure out your drink. Something basic and manly. No frills. Outdoorsy."

He liked that description. "Go on."

"Something strong. Maybe tequila. Are you the kind of guy who likes to get blitzed?"

An odd question. Even more strange was the way her attitude shifted from playful to serious, as if probing for a deeper answer. "I'm not a drunk."

She held out both her fists. "Suppose in my right hand, I had a magic pill that would give you energy. In my left is one that makes you sleep. Which would you choose?"

"An upper or a downer." He closed his hands over both her fists and pulled them together. "Neither. I like to be in control at all times."

Charlene bounced up beside them. "What's going on here? Ben, are you propositioning the help?"

"Go away, Charlene."

"You're such a grump." She made eye contact with Liz. "You'd be doing everybody a favor if you got this guy to lighten up. He really needs a woman."

Liz pulled her hands away from him. "That's not part of my job description."

"Speaking of uptight jerks," Charlene said, "Where are Patrice and Monte?"

"You don't want to see my sister," he advised.

"Oh, but I do. I want my chance to gloat."

The background music got louder and a couple of the women started dancing. Charlene shimmied toward them. When Ben turned back toward the bar, he saw an opened bottle of dark beer. The logo showed a sailboat scudding in the wind. "Good choice, Liz. It's my favorite drink."

"I knew somebody liked it." She poured the beer into a tall, frosted glass. "There were two six-packs in the fridge."

He settled onto a bar stool and spent the rest of the evening talking to Liz. Usually Ben kept to himself, but she was a good listener. He opened up. Spoke of his dreams, his love of the ocean and the purity of sailing in a hand-crafted wooden boat with a streamlined hull and perfectly designed sail—not unlike the wing of an aircraft—to catch the wind and soar.

Her green eyes shone with a steady light, encouraging him to wax poetic about the lure of open sea. "In a different era, I could have been a captain on a tallship."

"Or a pirate," she said. "A renegade."

"Aye, matey."

Though he probed, she avoided saying much about herself, claiming that her dreams generally revolved around mundane issues like paying her rent and having groceries. "What about your family?" he asked.

"Raised by a single mother." She shrugged. "Her only dream for me was that I'd find a man to marry me and take care of me. And her."

"You don't share that dream."

"Nightmare," she corrected. "I don't like people telling me what to do."

"Nobody does."

"Your family is a lot more interesting." She refilled his beer glass. "From what I hear, you're in the midst of the divorce from hell."

He wasn't surprised that she knew about Victoria. The staff overheard everything. Talk about his miserable marriage evolved into memories of better times. With his beloved daughter. With his grandpa.

Though their conversation was frequently interrupted by Charlene's friends, he and Liz seemed to be afloat on an island of calm. When he looked at his wristwatch, he could hardly believe that it was after one.

The party had begun to wind down. In a dark corner, Bloody Mary and Baldy carried on a breathy conversation with a lot of groping. Others played pool. Charlene swayed and danced by herself while Ramon watched with eager eyes.

Ben was surprised when Patrice and Monte joined him

at the bar. His sister was visibly upset, with makeup askew and eyes glowing like hot embers. She snarled at Liz. "Vodka and pomegranate juice in a tall glass. Make it a double."

"Same for me," Monte said.

"I didn't expect to see you down here," Ben said.

"Couldn't sleep," Patrice complained. "I can't believe Jerod intends to leave everything to that witch."

"We're family," Monte whined. "We deserve that inheritance. We need it."

Ben filled his mouth with beer to keep from commenting. His sister had a healthy annual income from trust funds, owned houses and cars and anything else her greedy heart desired. Not exactly living in the gutter.

"Maybe I should get pregnant." Patrice patted her concave belly. "Then Jerod would leave my child big bucks. The way he's done with your kid."

Anger clenched Ben's throat. "What about Natalie?"

Charlene sidled up to them. "She's the other big winner in the new will. A third for me. A third for your darling daughter. And the rest to be divided with dozens and dozens of others."

Beside him, Patrice scraped her fingernails on the bar. "The new will won't stand up in court. You tricked my grandpa."

"I love him," Charlene said. "That's something you wouldn't understand. Love. True love."

Ramon had appeared behind her shoulder. It didn't take a behavioral scientist to see that this conversation was about to turn nasty.

"Love?" Patrice spat the word. "Is that why you were humping Tony Lansing in the back hallway?"

Charlene tossed her head. "Just a congratulations kiss. No big deal."

Liz placed the drinks for Patrice and Monte on the bar. "Here you go, folks. Drink up. And settle down."

"Shut up," Patrice snapped. "When I need advice from a maid, I'll ask for it."

His sister closed her talons around her glass, and Ben guessed her intention. Patrice was about to throw her drink, just like a soap-opera diva. Before he could stop her, she let fly.

Charlene ducked.

Ramon got drenched.

Ben waded in to stop the scuffle. Fortunately, Liz had come around the bar and helped. Between them, they subdued the women and their partners.

Patrice and Monte flounced back up the stairs.

Charlene stood at the bar beside him. Her chest heaved as she breathed heavily. "Go to bed, Ben. I'm not going to do anything naughty."

He had absolutely no reason to believe her.

THOUGH LIZ HAD BEEN DRINKING nothing but ginger ale all night, she felt unsteady on her feet. It had been a long day; she was pooped.

The momentary adrenaline rush from the catfight between Patrice and Charlene faded in about two seconds. All she could think about was bed.

"Thanks for your help," Ben said.

"I've been in bar fights before." It almost pleased her to see these upper-crust snobs get down and dirty. "But this is the first time with people wearing Manolos and diamonds."

"You look tired. Time to close down the bar."

"I promised Rachel I'd stay until all these people went to bed."

"They're all spending the night. Could be here until dawn." He came around the bar to stand beside her and took the white towel she'd been using to wipe down the bar surface from her hand. "Allow me to escort you upstairs to your bedroom."

When she gazed up into his dreamy blue eyes, she had trouble focusing. For a second, she saw him in double vision. Two Bens. Twice as sexy.

Tired. She was so very tired. At the same time, a thread of arousal wove through her consciousness, making her aware of her own sensuality and awakening her guarded passions.

Allowing Ben to take her to bed seemed like a risky plan. Her defenses were down. She didn't want to take a chance on succumbing to her natural urges and dragging him into the bed with her. "I can make it on my own."

"I'm sure you can." A lazy grin lifted the corner of his mouth. "I was being polite."

Polite was the furthest thing from her mind. After seeing him in action, she wanted to feel those strong arms wrapped around her, to snuggle against his chest and drown herself in his masculine scent.

Enough. She lurched into action, dodging around him and heading for the staircase. "Good night, Ben."

By the time she reached her third-floor bedroom, her legs weighed a thousand pounds apiece. The inside of her head whirled like a mad carousel.

Collapsed across the narrow bed in her maid's garret, her last conscious thought was, Had she been drugged?

Chapter Six

The next morning, Liz eased from her bed. She moved slowly, very slowly. Her muscles creaked. She'd picked up a couple of bruises in her scuffle with Ramon—minor injuries that were nothing compared to the morning-after agony following a karate competition.

After a visit to the bathroom down the hall, she returned to her room, stripped off her stinky maid uniform and stretched. Knots of tension released with audible crackles. This stiffness and her groggy head reminded her of a hangover. But she hadn't been drinking.

Sucking the cottony insides of her cheeks, she *knew* that she'd been drugged last night. During the skirmish with Charlene and Patrice, Liz had been distracted. Someone could have slipped a narcotic into her ginger ale. Had it been Ben?

During the hours they'd spent talking across the bar, he hadn't seemed suspicious of her. The opposite, in fact. He'd shared his familial concerns and his memories. When he'd talked about sailing and being on the crew at the America's Cup, his voice had turned wistfully poetic, warm and so charming that she'd wanted to share his dreams, to sail away with him.

She had to stop thinking of Ben with all those pastel, romantic sensations. *He's not innocent. I saw him make a drug buy.*

But had he drugged her? It didn't make sense.

If someone had slipped a Mickey Finn into Liz's ginger ale, the more likely suspect was Charlene. That woman was up to something, and Liz wanted to know what. Before she started her second day as an undercover maid, she'd pay a quick visit to Charlene's bedroom. Though the blond bombshell wasn't the target of her investigation, she didn't like being manipulated…or drugged.

Dressed in a sleeveless maroon T-shirt and jeans, she crept barefoot down the staircase to the second floor. The smell of bacon and coffee wafted from the kitchen downstairs. Longingly, Liz gazed toward the staircase. She'd love a mug of dark French roast. At the dinner last night, her growling stomach had taught her an important lesson. Before she started serving everybody else, she needed to take care of her own needs.

Charlene's bedroom stood directly opposite Ben's. Their bedrooms flanked the end suite that belonged to Jerod. His door was ajar, and she heard Ben's voice coming from inside. Quickly, Liz turned the knob on Charlene's door and stepped inside—prepared to confront the blond diva.

Charlene wasn't there.

The curtains were drawn, and the queen-sized bed looked like it hadn't been slept in. Discarded clothing scattered haphazardly on the antique desk, makeup table, dresser and pink-upholstered lounging chair. This large room was cluttered with too much furniture. Like Charlene herself, the bedroom seemed greedy.

Liz's detective instincts told her that something was wrong. The general messiness felt different than the usual clutter left behind by a woman getting dressed for a party.

For one thing, the smell of perfume was overpowering. The open jewelry box on the dresser glittered in a flashy display. Diamonds? Was Charlene dumb enough to leave valuables lying around?

The stool in front of the makeup table had been overturned. The huge mirror surrounded by lights tilted at an angle, and the makeup containers were shoved back as though someone had leaned against the surface.

Liz imagined a struggle. Someone—like the hotheaded Ramon—might have forced Charlene backward against the makeup table.

Being careful not to touch anything and leave fingerprints, Liz tiptoed barefoot across the hardwood floor toward the dressing table. She stepped in a puddle, reached down to touch the wetness and held her fingers to her nose. The heavy floral scent made her eyes water.

The pink bottle of cologne lay on the floor where it had spilled. No way had Charlene left this mess. Not when she had a staff of servants to clean up after her.

Even if Charlene had gotten up early, she wouldn't have left her room this way. Liz suspected foul play; she needed to inform Ben immediately.

She stepped back into the hallway and entered Jerod's suite through the opened door. The sliding glass doors were open. Outside on the deck, she saw Jerod in his wheelchair with Ben and the nurse standing on either side of him. Ben wore a gray suit with a white shirt. His necktie was loosely knotted.

The moment she stepped outside, Jerod brightened. He

held out a hand toward her. "Get your butt over here, sweetheart."

Liz obeyed. When she took his hand, he pulled her closer with surprising strength. As she leaned down, she saw him take a couple of sniffs of the perfume. He closed his eyes and grinned. "Honey, you smell like a whole damn bouquet of roses."

"I guess I do." Obviously, he thought she was Charlene. His vision must be worse than anyone knew.

"Give me a peck on the cheek and run along. My nurse has got to take my blood pressure before Doctor Al gets here."

Liz didn't want to embarrass him by pointing out his mistake. Instead, she lightly kissed his cheek.

He beamed. "Thank you, honey."

BEN HADN'T REALIZED that Jerod's eyesight was so bad. Confusing Liz with Charlene? He must be nearly blind.

As Liz dragged him out of his grandpa's room and into the hall, he said quietly, "Thanks for playing along. Jerod won't start his day until he sees Charlene."

"Or smells her," she said as she looked him up and down. "You're all dressed up."

"I have a meeting with my divorce lawyers this morning. Not something I'm looking forward to." He looked down at Liz. Her jeans and T-shirt showed off her fine little body. "I like what you're wearing."

"Great," she said dismissively. "What time did you leave the party last night?"

"About fifteen minutes after you. I was bored into a stupor."

"Was Charlene still there? Did you notice anything strange about her?"

"She's always strange. What's this about?"

She pulled him into Charlene's room and closed the door. "Charlene might be missing. The bed doesn't look slept in. There are signs of a struggle."

He waved his hand in front of his face, trying to dispel the stink. "I've got to open a window."

"Don't touch anything. This could be a crime scene."

She illustrated her theory of a struggle by pointing out the position of the mirror, the messed-up bottles on the makeup table and the broken perfume bottle.

"Or," he said, "Charlene might be sacked out in someone else's bed."

"Does she sleep around?"

Ben thought for a moment. Though Charlene was an equal opportunity tease, he had no proof that she'd ever gone beyond a couple of kisses. "I don't think she's adulterous. But we both saw her playing Ramon against Tony last night."

"And her situation has changed."

He wasn't sure what she meant. "How so?"

"Jerod's will has changed. Charlene might behave differently."

Anger shot through him. If that gold digger planned to betray Jerod after conning him into leaving her his fortune, Ben would make sure she never saw a penny. He'd burn the damn house down before he let her inherit.

Liz said, "We should call the police."

"Not yet." His first concern was his grandpa. If Jerod found out that his beloved was messing around, it would break his heart. "First, we'll try to find her. I'll lock her bedroom door until we figure out where the hell she is."

Her eyebrows pinched in a scowl. "If we don't have an explanation in half an hour, we need to notify the sheriff. He'll want to talk to the witnesses before they leave."

"Witnesses?"

"I don't see traces of blood in here, but the CSI's can use luminol and—"

"Luminol? You sound like a TV detective show."

Suddenly defensive, she took a step backwards. "I've taken criminal law courses at school. I know about chain of evidence."

"Well, let's not hang out the yellow crime-scene tape just yet. There could be a simple explanation."

"I hope so."

Though she had obviously just crawled out of bed with her blond hair sticking out in wild tufts, she radiated intensity. Her bare feet, snug jeans and sleeveless shirt were cuter than hell, but the muscles in her well-toned arms flexed as her fingers drew into fists. She was a time bomb set to explode. "What's going on with you?"

"It's nothing." Her smile was forced. "You're probably right. There's a simple explanation."

Liz hoped her suspicions were groundless, but her instincts told her otherwise. This classy, beautiful mountain estate seethed with an undercurrent of hostility, jealousy and greed. At the center of every skirmish was Charlene. She'd argued with Ben about Jerod's care, battled Patrice about the will and whipped Ramon into a frenzy of sexual possessiveness. Liz feared the trophy wife might have pushed someone too far.

Downstairs, she snagged a cup of coffee and explained to Rachel that she had a few things to take care of before she put on her maid uniform and got to work. After her late-night stint at bartending, it only seemed fair.

A quick survey of the houseguests showed that Ramon

was missing. When she and Ben went to the parking area near the garage, they discovered that his car was gone. The most likely scenario: Charlene and Ramon had run off together.

Ben drained his coffee mug. "I guess that's it. The simple explanation."

"What about the struggle in her bedroom?"

"Passion." His jaw clenched. "Ramon and Charlene tussled in her bedroom before they headed out to find somewhere more private."

A plausible theory. But Liz wasn't completely convinced. Charlene might be a bimbo, but she wasn't a fool. She wouldn't do anything that might cause Jerod to change his mind about the will. "You have surveillance cameras at the front gate. Would the tape show Charlene and Ramon driving off together?"

"The cameras are on a twenty-four-hour loop. Not the most high-tech security available, but sufficient. We'll check."

As he marched up the asphalt driveway toward the gate, she had to jog to keep up. In contrast to his openness last night, anger had turned him cold. He'd do anything to protect his grandfather.

Inside the closet-sized security house beside the locked wrought-iron gates, Ben flipped open a metal locker door. Inside were an array of control switches and four small screens. He juggled a couple of switches.

"Pretty casual security system," she remarked. "Nothing is locked up."

"Mostly we use the cameras to monitor vehicles at the front gate. The visual image is transmitted to a couple of receivers in the house so we can see who we're buzzing inside."

"Not worried about burglary?"

"The only truly effective way to protect this much acreage requires dozens of cameras, sensors and monitors. Not to mention full-time security personnel. Never seemed worth the effort."

Typical. People seldom bothered with deadbolts, cameras and coded locks until *after* they'd experienced a break-in.

Ben pointed to the lower screen. "Here's the taping from last night." The time code on the lower right corner showed that at 9:32 p.m. Dr. Mancini drove to the gate, pressed the button to open it and left. In the passenger seat, she saw Tony Lansing, the lawyer.

The feed from two rotating cameras showed several hours of pastoral nighttime scenery. They fast-forwarded through sights of elk crossing the road and pine boughs tossing in the night winds. The view that encompassed the house showed a couple who had stepped outside for a smoke. Patrice and Monte came out to their vehicle and got something from the glove compartment. No one else entered or left.

In the tight space of the security shed, Liz leaned close to Ben's shoulder so she could see the screens. His suit coat still felt warm from the morning sun. Her hand lingered near the small of his back, but she hesitated to actually make physical contact. One touch might lead to another.

On the tapes, nothing happened until 11:47 p.m. when the screen went black.

Liz drew back. "A malfunction?"

He checked the controls. "It appears that the cameras were turned off."

"Can the controls be turned off from inside the house?"

"No," he said. "Only from here."

Her suspicions about foul play returned. Why else would the surveillance be deliberately manipulated? "If someone walked to the gates from the house or from the road outside, their approach would be seen on the surveillance cameras. Right?"

"There are blind spots," he said. "Especially along the fence line. And Charlene knew about them. She could have slipped away from the party and come out here."

The surveillance tape resumed at 2:37 a.m. Once again, the scene was peaceful.

"There." Liz pointed to the screen that showed the view of the house and the vehicles parked by the garage. "Ramon's car is already gone. If he left with Charlene, it wasn't caught on camera."

Ben shrugged. "Maybe we're making too much of this. Possibly, the cameras were down. Maybe some sort of electronic glitch."

"A very convenient lapse," she said. "We need to call the sheriff."

He turned and faced her. The walls of the tiny surveillance shed wrapped tightly around them. As she looked up into his eyes, her heartbeat accelerated. Too close. They were too close for her to ignore the attraction that sang through her veins.

He held her bare arms in a gentle grasp. "I need a favor, Liz. Don't say no until you've heard me out."

Unable to speak, she nodded.

"Jerod's health is my only concern. He loves Charlene. If she's run off with Ramon, my grandpa is the one who'll suffer."

"If he dies, she inherits." The words popped out before

she had a chance to censor her thoughts. She hadn't meant to speak lightly of Jerod's death.

Ben winced. His grip on her arms tightened. "Until I have a chance to check out Ramon and see if Charlene is with him, I don't want to involve the police. Maybe I can find her. Talk sense into her."

"I can't—"

"Please, Liz. Until I have this figured out, I need for you to remain silent."

She pulled free from his grasp. In this tiny space, she had nowhere to go. Even with her back against the opposite wall, his nearness confounded her.

He was asking her to betray her ethics, possibly to cover up a crime. As a private eye, she was duty-bound to report suspicions of wrongdoing to the authorities. As a law student, she knew her actions amounted to aiding and abetting.

Only two days ago, Harry Schooner had stuck her in a similar situation when he had refused to report the drug dealers. She'd waited until the next morning to contact a friend at the Denver PD and give him the location of the drug house.

Some decisions had to be based on the greater good. Protecting Jerod from unnecessary frustration and complication was important. She met Ben's intent gaze. "I'm not doing this for you. It's for Jerod."

The warmth of his smile was far more pleasing than it should have been. She hated herself for being so vulnerable.

"One more thing," he said. "Jerod needs to see Charlene again this morning. You could play that role. Tell him you're going into town and won't be back until later. Put his mind at ease."

"You want me to dress up like Charlene and deliberately deceive your grandfather?"

"To save him pain."

When he put it like that, how could she refuse?

Chapter Seven

Finally, she'd gotten into Ben's bedroom.

Ever since Liz had arrived at the Crawford estate, she'd been trying to sneak into his room and search for the illegal drugs she had seen him buy in Denver. She really hadn't expected him to be holding the door open and welcoming her across the threshold.

Together, they'd grabbed clothes and a wig from Charlene's room across the hall, but Liz had insisted on preserving the possible crime scene and had refused to change in Charlene's room.

Ben stood in the doorway. "Make sure you douse yourself in her perfume. That seems to be how Jerod recognizes her."

"Don't worry about me," she said. "Just keep Dr. Mancini and the nurse out of the room."

"No problem." He closed the door behind him.

She didn't have much time for a search. Not with Ben standing right outside. Every minute had to count. Tossing the platinum wig on the bed, she scanned the room. The style of the natural wood furniture was sleek, modern and somewhat bland—more like a hotel than a personal space. Apart from a few issues of *Wooden Boat* magazine on the bedside table, there was nothing of Ben. She reminded herself that this wasn't his primary residence; his real home was in Seattle.

Hiding drugs in the attached bathroom was too obvious so she concentrated on the bedroom, reaching into the backs of drawers and feeling behind furniture. Though she hated to mess up the bed, she slid her hand between the mattress and crawled underneath to check the box springs. So many hiding places, so little time.

As she dug through his closet, she threw on Charlene's tiny mini skirt and short-sleeved, pink cashmere sweater. Her instincts told her that this room was only the place where Ben slept. His drug stash was elsewhere.

After she settled the wig on her head, she stepped into the hallway where he waited. His eyebrows lifted at the sight of her, but he was smart enough not to tease. In a low voice, he said, "Charlene usually spends about fifteen minutes with Jerod."

"And what do they talk about?"

He shrugged. "The conversation is light. They laugh. He usually pats her bottom."

She looked over her shoulder. "I'm not built like Charlene. My butt might be okay, but if he reaches for my boobs, he'll know I'm a fake."

"You'll manage."

She didn't share his confidence. Undercover work usually involved being inconspicuous, but she would be trying to convince a man that she was his wife—someone he knew intimately. Her only advantage was that Jerod apparently saw her only as a vague outline.

With Ben keeping watch at the door so she wouldn't be disturbed, she entered Jerod's bedroom suite. He sat outside in his wheelchair on the deck. As she approached, she straightened her shoulders and put a bounce in her step. Since Charlene's shoes were a size too small, Liz remained barefoot.

She searched her auditory memory for the pitch of Charlene's voice, remembering a hint of Texas twang. Sidling up beside Jerod's chair, she used the pet name Charlene had spoken last night. "Howdy, bumblebee."

"Howdy yourself, honey." He turned his head toward her—his manner confident though unseeing. "Y'all have a good time last night?"

"Would have been better if you were there." Though Liz felt creepy about deceiving Jerod, she lightly laced her fingers with his and gave a squeeze. "What were we talking about yesterday?"

"Same as always. Family history. After I'm gone, you're fixing to be the head of the family. There's things you need to know." He frowned. "I sure as heck don't want you getting into more catfights with Patrice."

"But she's such a…" Liz searched for the right word. What would Charlene say? "Such a skinny witch."

"Go easy on her. She had a hard time after she lost her mama and papa in that damn car accident. That's when she told us not to call her Patty Sue any more. She was Patrice. Only fourteen years old and an orphan."

"That means Ben was…how old?"

"Sixteen. Sophomore in high school." Jerod leaned back in his wheelchair, giving up any pretense of looking at her. "He was as tall as he is right now. But scrawny as a wet barn cat. In the summers, the boy worked in the company oil business, and I'm proud to say he held his own with roughnecks who were twice his size."

"I'm confused." She fluttered her free hand in a gesture

she'd seen Charlene use. "The oil business was in Texas, but Ben settled in Seattle."

"I explained this before, honey. Ain't you been paying attention?"

"You know me." She fluttered again. "Gosh, I get ever so distracted."

His gnarled and weathered hand, still holding hers, tightened. "Don't you go playing the dumb blonde with me. We both know better."

Interesting. Apparently, there was more to Charlene than met the eye. "I never could fool you."

"Pay attention now. You hear me?"

"No need to be a grouch." The words slipped out before Liz could censor herself. She was accustomed to dealing with grumpy old Harold, who would ride rough-shod over her if she didn't stand up for herself.

"Huh? You think I'm grouchy?"

"Like a grizzly bear."

He chuckled. "That's my honey."

His posture relaxed as he bought into her performance. Apparently, Liz had more in common with Charlene than she'd thought. After they talked a bit more about the family and Charlene's new responsibilities as the matri-arch, Liz wrapped up their conversation. "I should get moving, bumblebee. After our guests clear out, I'm going shopping."

"Whatever you want." When he patted her butt, he frowned. "You been working out?"

"A bit." Liz stepped out of reach.

"Don't go getting too skinny," he said. "Take care of yourself. Your voice sounds like you might be coming down with a cold."

She darted forward and gave him a peck on the cheek. "See you later."

As she stepped through the bedroom and met Ben, she pulled off the blond wig. Looking at his solid, muscular body, it was difficult to imagine him as a scrawny teenager working the oil fields. "I like your grandpa."

"He's a good man, but too damned stubborn for his own good." In his left hand, he held a cell phone. "I called Ramon but got no answer. I'll drive into town and pay him a visit."

And she would go back to her maid duties. The disappearance of Charlene put a new wrinkle in her investigation, but her focus needed to stay clear: find Ben's drug stash.

The warmth of his smile made that search seem utterly repugnant. From all she'd seen of Ben, he was a good man. How could she ruin his chances for joint custody of his child?

"Thanks," he said, "for talking to grandpa. He doesn't need any more heartache."

He leaned closer. If she'd wanted to shove him away, she had ample opportunity. In no way was he forcing himself on her or taking advantage.

She should have objected. Instead, she tilted her chin up, welcoming his kiss. When his lips brushed hers, a brilliant flash of white heat exploded behind her eyes and blinded her to common sense. A burst of passion surged, forceful and challenging. She wanted the kiss to deepen and continue for long, intense moments. She wanted to know his body in every sense of the word. Her ferocious need for him felt unlike anything she'd experienced, as though they were destined to be together.

She had to be mistaken. Her instincts were dead wrong.

The maid and the millionaire? *No way.*

Reality was even worse. A detective and the subject of her investigation could not, should not, must not ever be involved on a personal level.

But as he moved away from her, she grabbed the lapels of his suit jacket and yanked him close, kissing him with all the wildfire passion that burned inside. His arms encircled her. The flames leapt higher.

She deepened the kiss, plunging her tongue into his mouth, and he responded with a fierce passion. His body pressed tightly against hers. She felt his hard arousal, and reveled in this evidence that she turned him on.

He felt the magnetism, too. They were a match. In spite of all their differences, they connected.

Oh, damn. This was all wrong.

WHEN BEN FINALLY LOCATED Ramon Stephens in the weight room at his posh Denver apartment building, Ramon was quick to point out the bruising on his shoulder and throat. "You did this to me, man."

He was lucky Ben hadn't torn his head off. "Where's Charlene?"

"I ought to sue." Ramon pouted. "I can't get any modeling jobs with bruises."

After canceling his lawyer's appointment and spending far too much time tracking this jerk down, Ben didn't have the patience to play games. He flipped the lock on the door handle of the weight room. No one else occupied the exercise equipment. "Where is she?"

"Damned if I know." Pumped from his workout, he checked out his reflection in the mirrors.

"What time did you and Charlene leave the party last night?"

"I left at around two in the morning. Alone."

He shrugged, sending a ripple across his pecs. All those muscles were impressive but served little purpose other than being decorative. This pretty boy looked like he'd never done an honest day's work in his whole life.

A long time ago in his grandpa's oil fields, Ben had learned what it meant to be a man, how to get what he wanted and how to fight for it. He also knew how to spot a liar. "There's something you're not telling me."

"Hey, man. I don't have to talk to you."

"Yeah. You do."

In a couple of simple moves, Ben had Ramon in a choke hold with his arm twisted up behind his back. "Did you leave with Charlene? Yes or no?"

"Let go of me."

When he wriggled, Ben hiked his arm higher. "Don't make me break your arm, Ramon. Answer my question."

"No. I didn't leave with her."

"Who did?"

"I don't know." His face in the mirror was an ugly grimace of pain.

"What are you hiding?"

"She dumped me. Okay? Is that what you want to hear? She told me to stay away from her. And I left."

Ben released his grasp and stepped out of range in case the pretty boy decided to retaliate. But there was no fight in Ramon. Cradling his arm against his chest, he sank to his knees and groaned.

Remembering the mess in Charlene's room and Liz's theory that there had been a struggle, Ben wondered if

Ramon had pushed Charlene around. "Did you go up to her room?"

"I tried. But no. I don't care about her anymore." He whimpered like a two-year-old. "I've got plenty of other dates."

No doubt, he was Mister Popularity. But that wasn't Ben's concern. "Who's Charlene's new boy toy?"

"The lawyer."

Tony Lansing, the attorney. His father had handled the Crawford family business for decades before passing the mantle. When Tony had taken over five years ago, Ben hadn't been impressed but hadn't expected any major problems. Jerod had sold his oil fields. No lawsuits were pending. Tony should have been able to handle the personal business.

As he walked out the door, Ben reached down and patted Ramon's shoulder. "Might want to ice that elbow."

DRIVING BACK INTO THE MOUNTAINS, Ben's frustration level grew. As he crested the last hill on I-70 before his turnoff, the panoramic view of the Rocky Mountains failed to lighten his mood. He wished himself back in Seattle where Crawford Aero-Equipment ran like clockwork. During his long physical absence in Colorado, his trusted vice presidents and supervisors kept production and sales on target. No need for worry.

It was his personal life that confounded him. His failed marriage. Jerod's illness. And now…Charlene's disappearance.

At the front gate to the estate, he punched the security code into the keypad. Why had the cameras been turned off from 11:47 until 2:37? The missing three hours indicated a premeditated plan. But not by Ramon.

There was no choice other than notifying the sheriff, but Ben needed to control the situation. He had strings he could pull, highly placed people who owed him favors. If possible, he intended to keep Jerod in the dark until they had everything figured out. Therefore, his first order of business was to talk privately to Liz and convince her to keep pretending to be Charlene.

The thought of Liz sent his mind racing off on a wild and not unpleasant tangent. Her kiss had surprised him. When he'd lightly tasted her sweet lips, he'd wanted more. But she'd turned out to be the aggressor. Of her own passionate accord, she had taken their connection deeper.

He needed to know more about Liz. In spite of her straightforward manner, he saw something mysterious about her. Just as he'd known that Ramon didn't want to talk about how he'd been dumped, he knew that Liz had a secret.

She was the first person he saw when he entered the house. Dressed in a maid uniform that fit marginally better than the one she wore yesterday, she flicked a feather duster across the back of a carved antique chair.

When she turned toward him, he placed a finger across his lips, indicating silence. Immediately, she dropped the duster and followed him outside.

"Did you find Charlene?" she asked.

He set off across the asphalt circle drive toward the log barn. They needed privacy for this conversation. "Ramon says he left by himself last night. I'm inclined to believe him."

"You didn't beat him up, did you?"

"Of course not." Just a little arm twisting.

"Where are we going?"

He pointed toward the one-story log barn. "I need to

make plans for how to handle Charlene's absence, and I want you to—"

"Call the sheriff," she said firmly. "The longer you wait, the more suspicious it looks."

"Suspicious?"

She jogged around in front of him, blocking his path and causing him to halt. "If something bad happened to Charlene, you're a suspect. You hated her."

"*Hate* is a strong word."

"Jerod's will was changed yesterday, and you were disinherited."

He scoffed. "I don't care about Jerod's money."

"That's not how it's going to look to the police."

He circumvented her and proceeded to the barn—the one place on this mountain property where he could go to calm his nerves. He plugged his key into the side door of the barn and shoved it open. Sunlight from high windows poured down on his woodworking shop and the partially completed hull of a twelve-foot-long sailboat he was building himself. Nothing in the world was more relaxing than sanding and smoothing the white oak planking.

Liz stepped past him into the barn as he hit the light switch. "A boat," she said.

"I plan to have it finished in a couple of weeks so I can take my daughter out on the lake and show her the basics of sailing."

When she looked up at him, her green eyes softened. "Every time I start thinking that you're nothing but a millionaire jerk, you pull something like this."

"Like what?"

"Something sweet and sensitive," she said as she

glided her hand along the satiny white oak surface. "Almost artistic."

At the stern of the boat, she came to a sudden stop. Her gaze aimed at the floor on the opposite side of the hull— a place he couldn't see.

"It's Charlene." Liz's voice trembled. "She's dead."

Chapter Eight

Liz had seen corpses before, at funerals and wakes, where the dead were displayed with carefully groomed hairdos, rouge and lipstick. Once in the city morgue, she and Harry had had to identify the remains of a client who had committed suicide. None of those prior experiences prepared her for seeing Charlene's body on the concrete floor beside Ben's boat.

In death, she seemed smaller and somehow flattened as if the air had deflated from her body, leaving a two-dimensional shell. Her eyes were half-closed. Her mouth gaped, and the rosy-pink lipstick contrasted with her waxen cheeks. The shiny blond hair that she loved to toss was matted with blood.

A piece of metal tackle, bloodied, rested beside her. It had to be the murder weapon.

Murder? Her knees wobbled. Her nerves clenched in a knot. For a moment, she forgot how to breathe. When Ben stepped up close behind her, she leaned against his chest, grateful for his support.

"Are you okay?" he asked.

"Fine," she replied automatically, not wanting her weakness to show. "Who would do this? Why?"

"I don't know."

She turned in the circle of his arms and clung to him. Inside his rib cage, she heard the steady thump of his heartbeat—an affirmation of life. His self-control and strength should have reassured her. Instead, she felt even more unnerved. "Finding her here. In your little hideout. It doesn't look good for you."

"I'm aware of that." His chest rose and fell as he drew in a deep breath and exhaled. "Other people have keys to this workshop."

"Who?" She choked out the word. "Who has a key?"

"The entire household has access. Rachel has duplicate keys to everything hanging on a labeled rack in the pantry."

"Then why bother to lock up?"

"A deterrent. I don't want my workshop turning into a place where the staff can come to grab a smoke and a beer. Or a place where guests can wander freely."

As he gently stroked her shoulder, she felt a trembling in his hand. From shock? From anger? She really didn't know a thing about him. They were barely acquainted. "This is a crime scene," she said. "We should get out of here."

Keeping his arm wrapped protectively around her waist, he escorted her to the door into the daylight. The perfect spring weather seemed like a travesty. She sucked down a lungful of the clean mountain air. Thankfully, her head began to clear.

Looking up at Ben, she studied the angles of his handsome face. His jaw was set firmly. The fine lines on his forehead deepened. Though she'd felt that tremor, the only evidence that he might be disturbed showed in his blue eyes. His gaze flickered. His lids blinked. *Wasn't that a sign of lying? Rapidly blinking eyelids?* Did he know more about the murder than he was saying?

"It's time," she said. "Call the sheriff."

"I don't think so." His brow furrowed as he took the cell phone from his suit coat pocket. "I'm going to start a bit higher up on the food chain."

"You can't orchestrate a murder investigation."

"Watch me," he said.

She stopped his hand before he could punch in a number. "I don't care if you have the governor on speed dial, you need to let the police do their job."

"I have no intention of standing in the way of an investigation, but I'll start with the Colorado Bureau of Investigation. I don't want a bunch of deputies running around here causing trouble."

"Heaven forbid they should make a mess," she said coldly.

"I'll handle this my way." His decision was made, and his voice took on the unmistakable ring of authority. Before her eyes, he transformed into a high-powered CEO—the sort of individual she'd spent most of her life resenting. He said, "I don't want Jerod to know what happened."

"There's no way you can keep Charlene's murder a secret."

"Everyone else will know. But not Jerod. God damn it." His voice cracked. "Not Jerod."

His arrogant facade slipped as the corners of his mouth tightened. "He's dying, Liz. Until this morning when he thought you were Charlene, I had no idea how bad his vision had become. He may have only a few weeks left."

Though she empathized with his feelings, she couldn't agree with his plan. "Jerod is weak, but his mental abilities are sharp. Even if you organize the most subtle murder investigation of all time, he'll know."

"You're right." He gazed skyward as if to search for answers in the wisps of clouds.

"You can't control this," she said. "All we can do right now is tell the truth."

"Jerod doesn't have to know…." She could almost see his mind working, analyzing the situation and coming to a solution. "He won't know if he's in the hospital."

"What?"

"With Charlene out of the way, I can convince Jerod to see my specialists."

With Charlene out of the way? In one callous phrase, he had dismissed the brutal murder of a young, vibrant woman. As if she were nothing more than an obstacle. "I can't believe you said that."

"About the specialists?"

"About Charlene. Her death counts, Ben." He couldn't just sweep her under the rug. Her murder needed to be taken seriously. "Yesterday, she was a living, breathing human being with dreams and schemes and hopes."

"And there were times when I liked her, when I believed that she loved my grandpa. She brightened his life, and I'm sorry that she's dead."

"A touching eulogy. I almost believe you."

"Now isn't the time for mourning. I need to handle the situation, and I need your help." He concentrated on her with a compelling intensity. "Will you help me, Liz?"

"To do what?"

"You'll impersonate Charlene one more time. Together, we'll see Jerod. Don't worry. I'll do most of the talking. I'll convince him to listen to reason and go into the hospital."

"Not a chance." She wanted no part of him or his plan. "I'll talk to the police, and then I'm out of here."

"What would it take to convince you? Money?"

Disgusted, she turned away from him. He was a different person. Gone was the wistful dreamer who talked of sailboats and sunsets. She saw no trace of the craftsman who had worked on the beautiful hull inside the workshop—the crime scene.

He continued. "I'd pay you enough to cover your law school tuition."

"This isn't about money," she said. "I won't lie to a dying man."

"Not even if your lie might save his life?"

Though she hated to admit it, he had a point. Jerod deserved the very best neurological care, and daily visits from Dr. Mancini, a retired general practitioner, didn't fall into that category. "I thought the main reason Jerod was here was because it was his preference, because he wanted to die at home?"

"It's been six weeks of slow deterioration—enough time that he might now change his mind if Charlene asks him to reconsider. You could give him this chance."

Ben wasn't someone she could trust; he trafficked with drug dealers. The staff thought he was a brooding loner. His estranged wife wanted to withhold custody of their child. But her instincts told her otherwise. She'd trusted Ben enough to kiss him. In his tone of voice, she heard nothing but sincerity; he truly cared for his grandpa. As did she. Jerod Crawford was a good person, and she wanted to help him.

She couldn't ignore the possibility that advanced medical care might save his life. "I'll do it."

PUTTING HER CONCERNS AND reservations on hold, Liz allowed herself to be swept into Ben's whirlwind plans. Cell phone in hand, he made rapid-fire calls as he tore through the house, pulling her in his wake. Through the door. Up the staircase.

Liz changed into the platinum wig. *God forgive me.* This was so wrong.

In his grandpa's bedroom, she played her role as Charlene, holding Jerod's hand and gazing into his nearly sightless eyes as Ben directed the conversation toward a new phase in Jerod's treatment.

When she spoke, her words stuttered. She was blatantly working a deception on a dying man, withholding the tragedy of his wife's murder. *He ought to know. He ought to be told.*

The only way she could get through this performance was to think of Harry Schooner and his unwavering refusal to take care of himself in spite of her concerns. If Jerod had been Harry, which really wasn't a far stretch of the imagination, she might be inclined to do the same thing Ben was doing with his grandpa.

Surprisingly, Jerod acquiesced to Ben's plan with hardly an objection, which made her think that he'd already been considering a similar action.

After she switched back into her maid uniform and stepped out of Ben's bedroom into the hall, she had only three words for him. "Nine. One. One."

"Not yet," he said. "The ambulance will be here in half an hour. Then I'll call in the police."

"Half an hour?" The last time she'd consulted a medical specialist about a knee injury, it had taken three weeks to make an appointment. "How did you make these arrangements so quickly?"

"I've had this plan in place for weeks, hoping Jerod would change his mind. The neurosurgeon will be waiting for the ambulance."

And how much would that cost? A new wing for the hospital? It certainly helped to have money, lots of money. Every procedure moved more smoothly when the road was paved with hundred-dollar bills.

AFTER JEROD WAS WHISKED AWAY in the ambulance, Liz watched as Ben made the calls to the authorities, to several people who owed him favors and to his attorneys. A complicated procedure.

Normal people rang up 9-1-1 and took whatever and whomever responded. Normal people had the common sense to step back and allow the lawmen to do their jobs. The rich, she realized, were different. And Ben was in a league of his own.

She couldn't fault his performance as he gathered the staff together with Patrice and Monte. He informed them all that Charlene had been murdered. "Liz and I found her body in the log barn."

"Are you sure?" Patrice asked. "She was murdered?"

"Yes," he said briskly.

Rachel seemed to be at a loss. Her large hands gestured clumsily. "What are we supposed to do? What are we supposed to say?"

Liz bit her lower lip to keep from snapping at her. *You're supposed to tell the truth. That's how murder investigations work.*

Ben said, "The police will be here shortly, and you're to cooperate with them."

Annette adjusted her maid cap and edged closer to the chauffeur. "Was it a serial killer? Are we in danger?"

Yeah, sure. A psycho killer just happened to show up at this remote estate and kill the most hated person on the premises. Liz glanced toward Patrice and Monte, who both seemed to be holding back whoops of joy. *Ding, dong, the witch is dead.*

"Oh, this is terrible," Monte said as he stifled his grin. "A real scandal."

"Does Jerod know?" Patrice asked.

"No," Ben responded. "And you're not to tell him. He's finally consented to seeing my specialists and needs to concentrate on getting better. He'll be told when the time is right."

Liz was dying to ask a few questions, maybe to do a quick interrogation before the police got here. Not that she had any authority to do so.

The chef wiped his hands on his white apron and stepped forward. "You mentioned that the police were on their way. Should I prepare something for them to eat?"

Liz couldn't help blurting, "Doughnuts."

All eyes turned toward her.

"A joke," she said. "You know, cops and doughnuts?"

Silence.

But now she had their attention. Might as well jump in. "When was the last time any of you saw Charlene?"

Everyone talked at once, recalling haphazardly their last encounter with the victim. Victim? Inwardly, Liz cringed. It was hard to think of the brazen, demanding Charlene that way.

The only person who remained silent was Annette. Her mousy, little face puckered, and her cheeks flushed a bright red.

Ben had also noticed her reticence. In a low, calm voice, he said. "Annette."

"Yes, sir." She jumped.

"Did you see something?"

"Yes, sir," she responded properly.

"Tell us about it."

"Well, it was very late." Her voice was thin and tiny. "When Liz came to bed, she made quite a lot of noise and woke me up."

"Sorry," Liz mumbled. Last night, she'd been reeling.

"Anyway," Annette said. "I couldn't get back to sleep. I thought maybe a beverage would help, so I went down to the kitchen." She drew a ragged breath. "While I was making my herbal tea, all the guests were going upstairs to the bedrooms. How very embarrassing. I didn't want to be seen in my bathrobe."

"Very proper," Rachel said approvingly. "The help should always be unobtrusive."

Ben shot a silencing glare in her direction and turned back to Annette. "Then what?"

"I went outside on the second floor deck where Mr. Jerod usually sits. There was a nice, thick wool blanket. So I curled up in a chair and drank my tea. I must have dozed off. Then I woke up. And I saw…" She covered her face with her hands and took a step back, away from Ben.

Liz went to her side and wrapped her arm around Annette's shoulders. The poor, meek, little thing was trembling. Had she witnessed the murder? "It's okay," she cooed. "Everything is going to be okay."

"I thought I was having a nightmare." Her eyes flooded with tears. "I saw a man carrying a woman down the hill and through the shadows. It was dark, and they were really far away. I couldn't see very well. It scared me. Like a monster movie."

"Nobody is going to hurt you." Liz pulled a crumpled

but unused tissue from her pocket and dabbed at Annette's tears. "You're safe now."

"The monster was carrying her toward the log barn."

"Can you describe him?" Liz asked.

With a loud sob, Annette collapsed against her. The tears gushed. "Can't say anything else. I can't."

For a few long moments while the traumatized girl sobbed uncontrollably, Liz simply held her. Her gaze linked with Ben's. In spite of his overbearing CEO demeanor, he seemed troubled and far more sympathetic to Annette's outburst than Liz. Patience had never been one of her finer qualities, and she was ready to shake Annette until the rest of her story fell out.

"Dry those tears," Liz said. "Concentrate, Annette. I need for you to tell us the rest of your story. What was the man wearing?"

"Excuse me," Patrice said coldly. "Why is the maid asking these questions? She has no authority to—"

"Leave her alone," Ben said. "Continue, Liz."

She nodded her thanks to him and repeated her question. "What was he wearing?"

"All black. Or dark blue." Gasping, she continued, "I think he had on a knit cap. In the moonlight, he looked huge."

"Like a monster," Liz said.

"It was awful. I was scared."

"Did you recognize him?"

"I'm not sure." She shook her head. "I can't be sure. Please don't make me say anything else."

"Here's the thing." She held Annette by the upper arms and confronted her. "The police will need to hear about this. You'll have to talk to them."

"No," she moaned. "It was only a nightmare."

"Start by telling us," Liz said firmly. "Who did you see? Who was the monster?"

Annette's arm thrust straight out, and she pointed. "It was Ben."

Chapter Nine

Two hours and thirty-seven minutes later, Ben sat behind the L-shaped teak desk in the downstairs study. The spacious, book-lined room—decorated in cool earth tones and equipped with computer, fax and file cabinets—was usually a quiet place. Not today.

Two attorneys from the firm that had been handling his divorce sat side-by-side on the cinnamon-colored sofa and argued with Tony Lansing, who perched on the edge of his chair and gestured emphatically. Patrice and Monte paced at the edge of the Navajo rug, occasionally tossing in commentary of their own.

The main topic at the moment was the handling of what promised to be a high-profile murder investigation. Surely, the press would be involved, and the family needed to be ready with a statement.

Ben wasn't listening. His fingers toyed with the mouse that rested on a Kermit the Frog mousepad that his daughter had given him for Christmas. One thought remained foremost in his mind: he wanted Liz to trust him again.

When Annette had made her semi-hysterical accusation that he had carried the limp and lifeless body of

Charlene into the night like a monster from a horror film, he'd almost laughed out loud. Then he had looked into Liz's face. While the others had gasped in shock, her gaze had remained steady, and he had seen disappointment in her eyes. He had known what she was thinking—that he had purposely avoided calling the police. She thought he was a cold-blooded killer.

The two plainclothes detectives from the Colorado Bureau of Investigation seemed to have reached the same conclusion. They'd arrived a few minutes after the local sheriff. The argument over jurisdiction was brief; the CBI had taken charge.

While their forensic team had gathered evidence and removed the body, Agent Lattimer had questioned the staff and gathered names and phone numbers for all the guests from last night who had already gone home.

In his interview, Ben had accepted full responsibility for allowing the guests to leave, for tampering with the potential crime scene in Charlene's bedroom and for not informing the police when he first suspected she might be missing. He had told the truth. Sure, he'd played fast and loose with proper procedure. But he wasn't a murderer.

The door to the study opened, and Rachel stepped inside. Her broad body eclipsed Liz, who followed behind her carrying a silver serving tray piled high with plates of little sandwiches and bowls of fresh fruit.

In her maid uniform, Liz seemed uncomfortable as usual. She'd given up on fastening the starched white cap into her sandy-colored hair. Though he stared at her, she didn't return his gaze.

After she placed the food on the coffee table, she approached Ben behind the desk. Reaching into her pocket, she took out a folded scrap of paper, which she slid across the desk toward him.

He flipped the note open. The slanted handwriting seemed to have been penned in haste. Likewise, her thoughts were in shorthand.

I quit. Heading back to Denver. My best to Jerod.
Liz.

He didn't want her to go. He needed her. She was his touchstone, his connection with reality in an increasingly unreal world. Her snippy attitude provided exactly the right antidote to the poisonous spewing of verbiage from the lawyers.

"Wait," he said as he rose from his chair.

The discussion fell silent. Rachel and Liz paused near the door.

Ben paced around the desk. The time had come to put an end to this legalese yammering. "Patrice will be our media spokesperson."

"Me?" Her eyelashes fluttered. "I couldn't."

"You'll do fine." And she already had the appropriate clothing for a mourner. Most of her wardrobe was black. "We'll need a written statement expressing our sorrow and our willingness to cooperate with the authorities."

Tony stood. "I'll get right on it."

"Not you." Ben hadn't forgotten last night when the family lawyer had been kissing Charlene in the hallway behind the kitchen. "Matter of fact, I want you out of here."

Tony stuck out his closely shaven chin and frowned in an attempt to show grave concern. "May I remind you," he said, "that my firm has represented the Crawford family for decades."

"Not anymore."

"Before you fire me, keep in mind that I know about all the skeletons in the family closet. I know the terms of Jerod's latest will."

"Big deal," Patrice said. "We all know that Grandpa was going to leave the bulk of his estate to Charlene. Obviously, that no longer applies."

"You don't know all the terms of the will," he said with a smug little grin. "There's a section about what happens if Charlene predeceases Jerod. And the terms don't look good for Ben."

Patrice darted across the room and stood before him. "With Charlene dead, everything ought to go back to the way it was before. An even split between me and Ben."

"Not at all." He preened. "Charlene's death means that her share of the estate will go to…Natalie."

"Ben's daughter?" Patrice trembled at the verge of tears. "That can't be. She's only a child."

One of Ben's divorce lawyers, a slender brunette with her hair pulled back in a bun, spoke up. "That information raises a number of concerns. The custody and guardianship of Natalie will be worth millions."

"For the last time," Ben said, "I don't care about the money."

His brunette lawyer made a clucking noise in the back of her throat. "In the midst of a divorce, many people make decisions that they later regret. That's why you hired us. We're here to protect your interests."

Her partner added, "And Tony's right. This looks bad for you."

"Why?"

"Motive," said the brunette. "Charlene's death means millions for your daughter. And for her legal guardians."

"Let's make one thing clear." Ben's gaze rested on Liz, who frowned and stared at her shoes. "I didn't kill Charlene. I didn't harm one single hair on her platinum-blond head."

"So," Tony said. "Am I fired?"

"Certainly not," Patrice said as she glared at Ben. "Let's get working on that statement. I need to be prepared."

Ben stalked toward the door, hooked his arm through Liz's and headed across the front room to the deck. As they went through the sliding doors to the outside, he kept a firm grasp.

She balked. "Take your hand off me."

"I want to make sure you won't run away."

"Let go," she growled. "Now."

Remembering her energetic demonstration of the knee-to-groin move, he released her. "I don't want you to quit."

Bristling, she strode to the railing at the edge of the deck into the mid-afternoon sunlight. This large cedar deck formed the center tier. Above them was Jerod's bedroom, with the best view of the lake and surrounding trees. Below was the stone terrace outside the party room with the bar.

He stepped up beside her and leaned his elbows on the railing. A soft wind brushed the buffalo grass and wild-flowers on the slope leading to the lake, but the serenity of the mountain valley was disrupted by a van that had driven down to the log barn. A couple of men in dark jackets with the letters *CBI* stenciled on the back slowly paced up the hill, staring at the ground.

"What did you tell the detectives?" she asked.

"The truth. I mentioned that you were in favor of notifying the authorities from the minute you noticed Charlene hadn't slept in her bed."

She nodded. "They weren't real happy with me for not using my own little fingers to dial 9-1-1."

"I put you in a difficult position," he said. "And I apologize for that."

"Don't worry about protecting me."

"Somebody needs to worry about you, Liz. Might as well be me."

"I can take care of myself, thank you." Her mouth puckered in a tight bow. "How's Jerod?"

"The doctors are still running tests. They won't know until tomorrow if he's a good candidate for surgery." He pointed to the two CBI investigators who were walking up the hill, occasionally pausing to take photographs. "What do you think they're doing?"

"Looking for the path that Annette's monster took when he was carrying Charlene. They might find evidence. A fiber or a footprint."

Another clue that would point to him as the primary suspect. He walked from the house to the log barn at least once every day.

He caught her gaze and held it. "Do you think I killed her?"

"I ought to believe it. Every bit of evidence, every action, every motive points to you." Her hand clenched into a fist, and she hammered on the railing. "You manipulated me. You kept me from calling the police, convinced me to lie to a dying man. I have absolutely no reason to believe in your innocence."

"But do you?"

He waited. Her opinion mattered more to him than the CBI and the lawyers.

"I don't believe you killed her."

"Good." For the first time in hours, his tension eased. But when he reached toward her, she batted his hand away.

"I'm not staying, Ben. I quit. I'm gone."

She darted across the deck and through the sliding glass doors. As he watched her disappear into the house, he promised himself that this would not be the last time he saw Liz Norton. For reasons he couldn't explain, she'd become important to him. He wouldn't let her go. Not without a fight.

A FULL DAY HAD PASSED, twenty-four long hours. Liz had slept for most of that time. Actually, she'd tossed and turned on her bed, torn by conflicting emotions.

Now, she parked her beat-up Toyota on the street outside the two-story stucco house that belonged to Victoria Crawford, Ben's estranged wife. She scowled at Harry, who sprawled in the passenger seat. For the past half hour, she'd been talking nonstop, giving a full report on what had happened at the Crawford estate.

Harry had said nothing. Behind his sunglasses, his eyes were probably closed. At least he wasn't snoring.

"This is the address," she said.

"Nice place, don't you think?"

In a glance, she took in the carpet of green lawn and tidy shrubbery. The red tile roof and elaborate iron latticework gave the impression of an urban villa. Before spending time at the palatial Crawford mountain estate, she would have been impressed. Now she had a new standard of opulence.

"Cute house," she said. "I still don't understand why we're here."

As far as she was concerned, her P.I. assignment had been a total bust. She hadn't found evidence that Ben was a drug user, had been a disaster as an undercover maid and had ended up knee-deep in a murder investigation.

Though she hadn't lied to the CBI detectives, she had most certainly withheld the fact that she worked for Schooner Detective Agency. Rachel had begged her not to say anything unless directly confronted, and Liz had complied with her wishes.

She hadn't told Ben, and she regretted her deception. While she'd been accusing him of lying and manipulating her, she'd been equally guilty. Probably more so.

The CBI Investigators hadn't pressed her for background information. Apparently, she wasn't a suspect. Only a maid. Putting on that uniform had made her invisible—even to the cops.

"We're here," Harry said, "because Mrs. Crawford paid us a good-sized retainer, and we want another big payday."

"But I didn't get what she wanted. I wasn't—"

"Let me do the talking." He pushed open the car door. "And try not to let her see that you've got the hots for her almost ex-husband."

"I do not."

He lowered his dark glasses and peeked over the rim. "Every time you say his name, you start drooling. Lovesick. That's what you are."

"Wrong, wrong, wrong. I can't stand guys like him. Arrogant, rich people who think they run the world. Ben lawyered up before the cops got there. I hate that."

With a groan, he hauled his bulk out of her car. "It

figures that when you finally get yourself hooked with a new boyfriend, he's a murder suspect."

"Ben is not my boyfriend," she said as she chased him up the sidewalk to the front door.

The woman who opened the door and graciously introduced herself to Liz as Victoria Crawford looked like a supermodel. Tall—nearly six feet—and skinny with shiny, shoulder-length black hair. Her casual summer walking shorts and tasteful jewelry looked like she'd stepped out of a *Vogue* photo shoot.

She swept Liz with a glance and said, "Rachel tells me you're not much of a maid."

"No, ma'am," she said, following Rachel's instructions for proper response.

"She did, however, say that you were handy to have around. You broke up a knife fight with Ramon and Tony?"

"Yes, ma'am."

"And spent the night bartending?"

Liz nodded. The repetition of *ma'am* was wearing on her nerves.

"And you seem to have done the impossible. You got Ben interested in you."

"Not really." Well, this was uncomfortable. What was the correct response to the estranged wife? Liz had never played the role of the "other woman" before.

"Don't bother to deny it." Victoria led them into a charming, antique-furnished living room. "I've moved on. My only interest in Ben is the size of his…wallet."

"Speaking of wallets," Harry said as he settled his bulk in a brocade chair. "How would you like for us to proceed with our investigation?"

"I want Liz to go back to the house and resume her undercover role as a maid."

Victoria's request was the last thing she had expected. "Why?"

"You're a detective, aren't you? And now there's a murder to investigate." She lifted her chin and looked down her nose. "I'm quite sure Ben is responsible for Charlene's death. He despised her. And he was seen carrying Charlene's body to his workshop. He's building a wooden boat, isn't he?"

"Yes."

"God, how I hate those woodworking projects of his! Always tinkering around, redesigning the hull, sanding the frame. He can afford a massive yacht with all the amenities. Why waste countless hours on something no bigger than a dinghy?"

Liz knew the answer. Ben enjoyed working with his hands, dreaming of the endless sea while he created his own craft. His woodworking project endeared him to her, made him less like a CEO and more like a regular guy.

Victoria turned toward Harry. "I will pay the balance of our contract after Ben is arrested for murder."

"Wait." Liz couldn't agree to those terms. "What if he didn't do it?"

"Liz brings up a good point," Harry said. "It might turn out that someone else is the killer."

"In that very unlikely case, I will honor our contract."

"So we get paid," Harry said. "Either way."

"Exactly so." Victoria rose to her feet and checked her wristwatch. "I hate to rush you off, but Dr. Mancini will be here at any moment. Natalie has the sniffles, and he agreed to stop by for a visit."

"Mancini?" Harry frowned. "Isn't that the same doc who was treating Jerod Crawford?"

"Family doctor. Natalie likes him." She glanced between them. "Are we agreed?"

Liz hated this plan. "Why should I pretend to be a maid? Since you want me to be a detective, I should go there as a private investigator."

"In an undercover position, you'll find out a lot more. Ben won't trust you for a moment if he knows you're working for me."

"At least, it would be the truth."

Anger glittered in Victoria's eyes. "I'm not paying for the truth. I want Ben charged with murder so I get sole custody of our daughter."

And complete control of the inheritance?

A bitter taste prickled on Liz's tongue. She didn't want to work against Ben. She liked him, and she didn't believe he was a killer. The only way this could turn out right was for her to prove her conviction.

Chapter Ten

Later that evening, alone in her one-bedroom apartment, Liz stared out her third-floor window at the Dumpsters in the alley and street lamps shining on the asphalt parking lot. When she'd stood on the cedar deck beside Ben, she'd seen snow-covered peaks, forests and a shimmering lake—a million-dollar panorama. The view from her apartment was worth about a buck twenty-five.

She contemplated the three withered houseplants lined up in a row across her windowsill while she pondered the ethical problem of returning to the Crawford estate. Harry wanted her to do it, wanted the big payoff from Victoria and didn't see anything wrong with her going there.

According to him, all she had to do was play her role as a maid—set the table and flick a feather duster until the CBI did their job and arrested someone for Charlene's murder.

Though she hated the idea of merely hanging around and watching, Harry probably had it right. All she needed was patience. The real issue—the problem that tied her gut in a knot—was that she'd be lying to Ben. Again.

She turned her glare on the deceased plants in their

plastic containers. This feeble attempt at beautifying her home had come during the dead of winter when the days had been short and everything had felt gloomy. During finals, she'd forgotten to water them.

At the well-run Crawford estate, the petunias in the flower box on Jerod's deck would never be allowed to shrivel. After experiencing firsthand how the upper one percent lived, her hand-to-mouth lifestyle seemed shabby—and yet, blissfully simple. She didn't need a chef, chauffeur, housekeeper and maids to keep her household running. No attorneys. No family doctors.

She was on her own and liked it that way.

Grabbing a black plastic garbage bag, she dumped the dead foliage. Simple. Problem solved.

She flung herself into the big, comfy reading chair— the only real piece of furniture in her front room, which was set up as an office with a huge desk for her computer and research papers, lots of bookshelves and a beat-up entertainment center. Maybe if she made a list of pluses and minuses, she could decide.

Resting a legal pad on the knees of her black yoga pants, she scribbled reasons why she shouldn't go back.

Number one: incompetence. She was a lousy maid.

Number two: pride. She'd stormed out the door earlier. How could she return without looking like a jerk?

Number three: danger. No matter how lovely the estate, there was a murderer on the loose.

Number four: Ben. She wrote his name twice, underlined and put a row of exclamation points at the end.

When he wasn't acting like a pushy CEO, he intrigued her with his stories about flying solo and crewing for the America's Cup. His selfless concern for his grandfather was admirable. In capital letters, she wrote the word *sexy*.

She groaned. It was crazy to think that there could ever be anything between them. Men like Ben hooked up with statuesque supermodels like his estranged wife.

She scratched through his twice-written name, then cross-hatched and scribbled over the letters again.

A knock at the door startled her. Leaping from her chair, she peeked through the fisheye and saw him. Ben.

He hadn't buzzed from downstairs, but that wasn't unusual. People were always walking in and out of this three-story building, and nobody bothered to ask for I.D.

He knocked again. She could pretend not to be home, avoid the problem for as long as possible. But she wasn't a coward.

Flipping the door lock, she opened wide.

"Thanks for seeing me," he said.

"Do I have a choice?"

"May I come in?"

She glanced over her shoulder at her drab little apartment and squashed the impulse to apologize. She didn't need his approval. "You've got five minutes."

When he walked through the door, he filled up her apartment with his masculine energy. During the two years she'd lived there, she'd probably had only three male guests. None of them compared to Ben. Surprisingly, he didn't look out of place. Though his suit probably cost more than her semester's tuition at law school, he'd been under stress and looked as rumpled as the Dumpster divers who patrolled her alley.

She perched on the swivel chair beside her computer and pointed to the big, comfy armchair. Ben filled the space nicely. Too nicely.

Abruptly, she said, "What do you want?"

"You always jump right in. Ask the hard questions."

When he grinned, the whole apartment lit up. Her seventy-five-watt bulbs blazed like spotlights. "When we met, you asked, Who loves you?"

Me, she wanted to shout. *Wrong*. She was too smart to fall for a guy she could never have. "Got an answer?"

"To which question?"

"Why are you here?"

"I want you to come back to work for me," he said. "I have two reasons. The first is Jerod. I want you to play the role of Charlene."

"He still doesn't know that she's dead? The murder has been all over the news. Patrice almost looks like she's really in mourning with that black dress."

"The pearls are a nice touch," he agreed.

"Why hasn't Jerod seen it?"

"Since he's been in the hospital, they've kept him busy with tests. Mostly, he's been sleeping." He leaned forward, and his hair fell across his forehead. Absently, he pushed it back. "It's likely the doctors will operate tomorrow. I don't want Jerod to be jolted by this tragedy when he's going into surgery. He needs a reason to live."

Though she didn't approve, she understood. "And the second reason you want me back?"

"The murder investigation. It's possible that you're the only person who believes I'm innocent." His blue eyes shone with a sincerity she really wanted to believe. "The only way I'm going to get out of this in one piece is to solve the crime myself. And I want you to help me."

Solving a real crime? A tickle of excitement raised goose bumps on her forearms. In all the time she'd been working for Schooner Private Investigations, the closest she'd gotten to sleuthing was tracking down an unfaithful husband who wore a fake mustache when he met his mistress. Being involved in a real investigation? She liked the idea, liked it a lot.

"I'd pay you," he said.

"Not necessary." She was already getting paid by Victoria who, ironically, wanted exactly the same thing as her estranged husband: to find Charlene's murderer.

He reached down and picked up the legal pad she'd discarded on the floor. "Interesting list," he said. "Incompetence. Pride. Danger. And sexy? Sounds like the plot for a soap opera."

She yanked the pad from his hands. "That's mine."

"What's the word you scratched out?"

"None of your business." She felt herself blushing again. Whenever she was around him, she got flushed and her cheeks turned scarlet. *Way too sexy.* Flipping the page on her legal pad, she picked up her pen. "We need a list. First issue. Who turned off the surveillance at the gate? And why?"

"I assume this marks the start of the investigation," he said. "*Our* investigation."

"Guess so."

He came toward her. Resting his hands on the arms of her swivel chair, he leaned down and lightly kissed her forehead.

Now she was blushing all over, which wasn't something she wanted to share with him. She shoved at his chest. "Don't get all mushy. I could still change my mind."

His smile communicated a warmth and appreciation that could never be expressed in words. "You're right, Liz. We should get down to business. Bring your legal pad, and let's go."

She lurched into her bedroom to throw some clothes

and a couple of changes of underwear into a gym bag. Ethically, everything had fallen into place. Except for the tiny problem that she was being paid by his estranged wife.

WHEN LIZ HAD DONE HER IMPERSONATION of Charlene in Jerod's private room at the hospital, Ben had almost been jealous of the way she'd lavished attention on his grandpa. With whispers and giggles, she'd teased Jerod. Willingly, she'd given him a good-night kiss.

That sure as hell wasn't the way she treated Ben. With him, her shields were up.

As he drove west toward the mountains, she still wore the low-cut red silk shirt that she'd used for her Charlene persona, but she'd covered up with a denim jacket. Scowling, she complained, "I still think I should have taken my own car."

"We'll be in and out of Denver every day to see Jerod. Tomorrow, you can get your car. I want to use this drive time to create a strategy for our investigation."

"Multitasking. I'll bet you're a good CEO."

"It's what I do."

"Okay, let's not waste any more time." She wriggled around in the passenger seat, turned on the roof light and dug around in the back of his Mustang. When she returned to her seat, she had the legal pad in hand. "We need a list of suspects."

An obvious first step. Finally, he was with someone who was ready for action. After all the suspicion, innuendo and hand-wringing, he welcomed a task he could sink his teeth into. "Since the surveillance at the front gate was turned off, we can assume that Charlene's murder was premeditated."

"Which rules out a crime of passion," she said.

"Therefore, Ramon's story must be true. He wanted to get Charlene into bed, but she dumped him. And he left."

"With his tail tucked between his legs." She gave a sardonic chuckle. "I'm writing Ramon's name down, anyway. He's suspicious. And what about the third member of that love triangle?"

"Tony Lansing." Ben's intuitive distrust of the lawyer had grown deeper when Tony had threatened him about exposing the skeletons in the Crawford family closet.

"Is he an alcoholic?" she asked as she scribbled Tony's name onto her list.

"Not as far as I know."

"Two days ago, during dinner, he tossed back three straight vodkas and a bottle of wine. That's the kind of thing you notice when you're tending bar."

"Being drunk might explain why he was dumb enough to grope Charlene in a house full of people."

"Or he might have been drinking for liquid courage. Knowing that he'd come back later, turn off the surveillance camera and commit murder."

Accelerating with a satisfying roar from the Mustang engine, Ben exited the highway onto the access road. Though only a little after nine o'clock, it felt like midnight. Today had been hell.

"Tony had no motive," he said. "With Jerod's will leaving the bulk of his estate to Charlene, Tony had reason to romance her in the hope that she'd soon be a wealthy widow. He wouldn't want her dead."

"Good point." She made a note on her legal pad. "Still, it might be good to talk to him. Find out where he was on the night of the murder."

"No problem."

Tony had been adamant about his role as the Crawford family lawyer; now it was time for him to live up to that responsibility. Ben flipped open his cell phone, called Tony Lansing on speed dial and left a message on the answering machine about wanting to see him as soon as possible.

He disconnected the call. "I hope that ruins his evening."

"Ben, there's something I didn't tell you about the night of the murder. After I left the bar and went to bed, I was hammered. Dizzy and wobbling all over the place even though I hadn't had a drop of alcohol. I'm pretty sure I was drugged."

What the hell? He turned his head and looked at her.

Immediately, he was distracted from crime solving. Even in the shadowy light from the dashboard, she was cute. No matter how high she piled the chips on her shoulder, she still had a sweetness about her. Maybe it was the way her mouth turned up at the corners. Or her hair, that wild hair.

"Ben? Are you with me?"

"Right." He needed to stay focused. "Why would somebody drug you?"

"Don't know *why*." Her shoulders rose and fell in a shrug. "But I do know *how*. During the catfight between Charlene and Patrice, somebody could have slipped a powder into the ginger ale I was drinking."

"If you were drugged, it could mean—"

"If?" Her voice rose. "I *was* drugged. It's a fact. I know what it feels like."

"Do you take drugs?"

"Do you?"

"That's the second time you've asked that question.

And it's absurd. Are my eyes dilated? My speech slurred? Do I strike you as being out of control?"

"I wouldn't blame you," she said. "You might need a little something to take the edge off. Every now and then."

"My edge is an asset."

He needed to stay sharp to make business decisions. Running a multi-million-dollar company required acuity and the innate sense of responsibility he'd been born with. Even before his parents had died, he'd liked being in charge—learning from the ground up, analyzing, then taking control.

In that sense, he was much like his grandpa. More than wealth and privilege, Jerod's legacy to Ben was an ability to see what was needed, plan a course of action and succeed. "Let's get back to the suspects. *When* you were drugged, who was nearby?"

"Charlene. Ramon. Patrice and Monte."

"My sister and her husband need to go on the suspect list." He hated that undeniable fact. "Their motive is the changed will."

She made a note on her legal pad. "The timing of the new will can't be a coincidence. Within hours of its being signed and witnessed, Charlene was dead."

"Following that logic, the person who most benefits from Charlene's death is me. My daughter inherits the bulk of the estate."

As he turned onto the winding two-lane road that led to the house, the night closed more tightly around them. The facts weighed against him.

"Someone else benefits," she pointed out. "Your estranged wife."

"Victoria? She wasn't anywhere near the estate last night."

"We don't know that. The surveillance camera was off." She gestured with her pen. "But Victoria couldn't have been the person Annette saw carrying Charlene's body."

He wasn't so sure. Victoria was tall and in excellent physical condition. "Put her name on the list."

"I'll talk to Annette tonight and find out if her 'monster' could have been a woman," Liz said. "Her room is right next to mine."

Again, his concentration slid away from their list of suspects and refocused on the woman sitting beside him. Since her supposed job at the house was as a maid, she would, of course, stay in the upstairs quarters.

In the back of his mind, he'd hoped for a different sleeping arrangement. He wanted her closer to him, preferably in his bed.

As he came around a sharp turn at the foot of a forested slope, his headlights shone on an obstacle in the road. No way around it. He slammed on the brakes.

Chapter Eleven

Unable to come to a complete stop in time, the bumper of Ben's Mustang nudged the object in the road. He threw the car in Reverse, backed up.

His headlights shone on the carcass of a bull elk with a full rack of antlers.

"Did you kill him?" she demanded in the accusing tone of an outraged city girl who thought anything with fur and hooves was Bambi.

"Not enough impact." In a fatal collision between a seven-hundred-pound animal and his Mustang, the car would have been totaled. "He was dead before we got here."

"Hunters," she said in a tone that made it sound like a dirty word.

"They shouldn't be here. This area is off-limits, and hunting season is September."

"How do you know that date?"

"I hunt."

"Yuck."

After her kick-ass displays of karate, he didn't expect her to be squeamish. "What? Are you a vegetarian?"

"I eat meat," she said. "But it comes neatly packaged in the grocery store. Which is the way God intended."

He exited the car and slammed the door. The huge elk had fallen across a narrow spot in the road. On one side, the trunks of ponderosa pine came all the way up to the shoulder. The other side was a steep cliff. If they pushed the rear haunches aside, he could squeeze by on the rocky side.

Liz went to the head of the animal and looked down into the wide-opened eyes. "How could anyone take pleasure from killing such a beautiful creature?"

"For the meat." But this animal had been left behind with no attempt to harvest the venison. Not even the impressive rack of antlers had been taken. Ben couldn't imagine that the animal had fallen in the middle of the road. This carcass had been placed here. As an obstacle. For him?

The hairs on the back of his neck prickled. He sensed that someone was near, someone was watching. This was a trap.

"Get back in the car, Liz."

Fists on hips, she confronted him. "You're going to need my help to move him. He probably weighs a ton."

No time to argue. He started toward her.

The thud of a bullet hit the road near his feet. There was no sound of a gun being fired. Must be using a silencer.

He dived toward Liz and shoved her behind the car. He couldn't hear the shots but sensed them. A bullet shattered the dry bark on a tree trunk. Another tore through an overhanging bough. Close. Too close. Ben heard another whiz past his ear.

Liz's moaning about poor dead Bambi ended. She

ducked behind the car beside him. Her attitude was all action. "An ambush," she whispered.

"The shooter has to be up on the hill. It's a good vantage point."

She glanced over her shoulder into the forested hillside that sloped downhill. "How far are we from the house? Can we make a run for it?"

Not a chance. Running through the trees, they'd be easy targets for a sniper with a nightscope. He'd already missed three times. A fourth was too much to hope for. "We're better off in the car."

"Can you go back the way we came?"

"Going in reverse down hairpin turns?" He shook his head. "We'd have to go too slow. We'd be an easy target."

"Then we have to go forward. How can you get around the elk?"

"I'll have to drive over the back haunches on the side nearest the cliff."

She gave a nod. "Let's do it."

"Once you get in the car, stay down."

Moving fast, he climbed through the passenger side and into the driver's seat. If he'd taken the SUV with the higher undercarriage, getting past the carcass wouldn't have been a difficult obstacle. With the Mustang, he had to count on the power of eight-cylinder acceleration. He'd make it. His engine had the juice.

He cranked the ignition and took off. With a sickening bump, the tires went over the back legs. Momentarily out of control, the Mustang skidded toward the rocky cliff. Ben flipped the steering wheel to straighten the nose.

Speed was his forte. Whether in a plane or boat or car, he knew how to go fast. Maneuvering on sheer instinct, he whipped along the winding road.

He heard no shots and felt no impact. None of the windows shattered. They were home-free.

Liz peered up over the dashboard. "Are you okay?"

"Fine. You?"

"I'm good."

Adrenaline poured through him, and his pulse raced. The thrill of making a good escape from a dangerous situation lifted his spirits. They were damned lucky to have gotten away from the sniper without a scratch.

And there was another positive aspect to this incident. Having the murderer come after him ought to alter the suspicions of the CBI investigators.

On the down side…somebody wanted him dead.

DANGER. LIZ HAD WRITTEN THE word on her legal pad when making her decision about coming back to the Crawford estate. A murderer was, by definition, a dangerous person. But she hadn't expected an ambush, a sniper on the hillside and a dead elk. Someone had tried to kill Ben. Or her. Or both of them.

A hint of fear nibbled at her consciousness, but she wasn't really scared as they swiveled around hairpin turns on the narrow mountain road. Ben handled the Mustang like a Grand Prix professional. "You're a good driver," she said.

"I know."

"Any idea who wants to kill you?"

"Not a clue."

When he cruised through the security gates, she noticed a difference in the cedar-and-stone house with cantilevered decks. Though illuminated by moonlight, the shadows dominated. Most of the windows were dark. The house reminded her of a bleak empty shell.

Jerod was gone.

Charlene was dead.

The only people in residence were Patrice, Monte and the staff. It seemed they had all gone to bed and pulled the covers over their ears.

After Ben parked the Mustang near the front door, he reached over and rested his hand on her shoulder. His touch was electric, sparking a sense of tension and exhilaration. "Liz, are you sure you're okay?"

"I'm not afraid," she said honestly. "Maybe a little startled. For a few minutes, things got kind of hairy."

"If you don't want to be a part of this, I'll understand." Sincerity resonated in his baritone voice. "We can arrange for you to ride back into Denver with one of the cops."

"I'm not leaving." She rested her hand on top of his. "Not now. The situation is starting to get interesting."

When he smiled, his blue eyes flashed with excitement, and she recognized a kindred spirit—a man who, like her, never backed away from a threat.

She and Ben came from opposite ends of the social scale. He was an arrogant CEO. She scraped by as a struggling law student and part-time private eye. He drove a Mustang as his second car. She bounced along in an aging Toyota. Their differences were myriad. And yet, at their core, they meshed perfectly. Both of them welcomed challenge. Stubborn and kick-ass, they made quite a pair.

Plucking his hand from her shoulder, she reached for the door handle on the Mustang. "Let's concentrate on finding the killer."

"I'll call the CBI."

"And we need to check on the people in the house. To make sure none of them are moonlighting as a sniper."

Inside the house, they turned on lights and made plenty

of noise. She trailed Ben into the study, where he found the phone number of the CBI agents working the case and made his call.

Rachel Frakes, wrapped in a navy flannel bathrobe patterned with white moose, poked her head through the door. Her usually slicked-back hair fell softly around her cheeks, but her eyes were hard and cold as she stared at Liz. "What on earth are you two doing?"

Ben answered, "Somebody shot at us on the road. I want you to check on the chef, gardener and chauffeur. Make sure everyone is accounted for."

"Yes, sir."

She fired another glare at Liz before turning on her heel and stalking from the room. For such a big woman, she was incredibly light on her feet.

While Ben barked into the phone, Liz moved toward the hallway, thinking that she'd peek into Patrice's room. Though it was hard to imagine that chic, black-clad shrew perched on a hillside with a sniper rifle, her husband might be capable of opening fire on Ben. According to Annette, Monte was an Olympic marksman.

"Wait," Ben said. "Where are you going?"

Over her shoulder, she said, "I thought I'd see what Patrice and Monte are up to."

"Give me a minute. I'll go with you."

While he returned to his phone call, she loitered in the doorway, half in the study and half out. At the far end of the hall, she glimpsed a ghostly form. Who was it? What was it?

Liz rushed down the hall and encountered Annette. With her long, heavy brown hair pulled back in a braid and a flower-sprigged flannel nightgown that fell all the way to the floor, she resembled a Gothic heroine from days gone by.

"What are you doing here?" Annette asked. "I thought you quit."

"Changed my mind."

"Fickle."

Now was as good a time as any to start acting like a real homicide detective. Liz had a lot of questions for this sweet young woman who claimed to have seen Ben carrying Charlene's lifeless body toward its final resting place.

Liz offered an encouraging smile. "How are you doing, Annette? It's been a traumatic couple of days for you."

"As if you give a damn."

Her lower lip pushed out in a frown. Somehow, Liz needed to gain her trust. Empathy usually worked. "It must have been terrifying to see that monster."

"Yes, it was." Still scowling, she folded her arms below her breasts. This hostility was puzzling. Annette had no reason to hate her.

"You were out on the deck. All alone," Liz said. "Why didn't you call for help?"

"How could I know Charlene was dead? I thought they might be playing games. You know, sex games."

Liz glanced over her shoulder toward the study and lowered her voice. "Does Ben do that kind of thing?"

"Well," she huffed, "you ought to know."

"Me?"

"I saw what was going on between the two of you. Sneaking off together. Giving each other little winks and nudges." She waggled a finger. "Mark my words. Ben won't fall for the likes of you. Ben has class."

When she spoke his name, she exhaled a wistful little

sigh. Apparently, Annette was a bit infatuated with the lord of the manor. Even if she thought he was a murderer.

Liz said, "There's nothing between me and—"

"Don't lie. You seduced him. That's why you're really back here, isn't it? To be his mistress."

Liz couldn't believe anyone would think of her that way. The only males who ever had crushes on her were the eight-year-old boys in the karate class she taught at Dragon Lou's.

Ben's mistress, huh? Was that the opinion of the staff? That she was sleeping with the boss, that she had employed her dubious feminine wiles to bag herself a millionaire? *Hah!* Her mother would have been so proud.

"Annette, I'm not having sex with Ben."

"Why else would he be interested in you? You're not especially pretty, you know."

"Thanks." This innocent little maid had a decidedly witchy streak.

"I'm not trying to be mean. But look at your hair. You're a mess."

"I don't bother much with my appearance," Liz said. "And I don't sleep with men I've only known for a few hours. Do you?"

"Never."

Her small face puckered, deepening the fine lines around her eyes and at the corners of her mouth. Though she acted like a third-grader, she might be older than Liz had supposed. She asked, "How long have you been a maid?"

"I've been with the Crawfords for almost a year. This is my first maid job."

"Do you like it?"

"Sometimes. I used to work at a hospital. Dr. Mancini said I should go back to school and get trained as a nurse."

"You'd make a good nurse." Liz slathered on the compliments; she wanted Annette to confide in her. "I've seen you at work. You're very precise. And clean."

Annette's mouth twitched as if she couldn't decide whether to sneer or smile. "Are you sure you're not sleeping with Ben?"

"Not that I recall, and I'd remember. He's a good-looking man, isn't he?"

"Oh, yes." She sighed.

Trying to wheedle her way into Annette's confidence, Liz offered more information. "Somebody's after him. While we were driving up here, a sniper set up an ambush."

"No!" She gasped. "You have to tell me everything."

At that moment, Ben stepped into the hallway. "Agent Lattimer is on his way with a forensic team." He nodded to Annette. "Did we wake you?"

"I was already up."

"You seem to do a lot of wandering around at night."

"I have insomnia." Her hands moved nervously across the flannel of her gown. Feverish color appeared in her cheeks. "Liz said that someone tried to shoot you."

"Yes."

His tone was curt. His attitude, dismissive. Liz couldn't fault him for being cold toward Annette. Her weird testimony about seeing him with Charlene's body had gone a long way toward making Ben a suspect.

To Liz, he said, "I'm going to rouse Patrice and Monte. I want them both present when the CBI is here."

She nodded. "And I'll need to give a statement."

Annette whispered, "Should I stay up?"

Without even looking at her, Ben said, "I don't care."

Obviously, he didn't appreciate the intensity of her in-fatuation with him. Annette was panting to be noticed. Taking pity on the wistful little maid, Liz caught hold of her arm. "Let's go upstairs together. I need to drop off my stuff."

On the third floor, Liz opened the door and tossed her gym bag into her garret-sized bedroom. Annette paused outside the room next door with her hand on the round brass knob. "Ben is angry with me, isn't he?"

Witnessing this unrequited affection pained Liz. She was fairly sure that Ben didn't care enough about Annette to be angry, sad, pleased or anything else. "Do you want to talk about it?"

"Yes," she said emphatically. "And you can tell me about the sniper."

She pushed open the door and invited Liz into her room. Spotlessly clean, the tiny bedroom sparkled with star-shaped ornaments hung from the rafters by invisible wires. The pine surface of the dresser held a crowd of cut glass figurines, several of which were fairy princesses. A framed poster from *Beauty and the Beast* dominated one wall.

Annette flounced into the center of the baby-blue com-forter on her single bed and beamed like a teenager at a slumber party. Had she cast Ben in the role of Prince Charming? Had she named him as the "monster" in a des-perate attempt to get his attention?

"Okay," she said. "Tell me what happened."

While Liz described the elk in the road and the sniper, Annette added her own embellishments, various descrip-tions that made Ben sound like a superhero.

"He's very courageous," Annette said. "And he's always been nice to me. Not like Patrice."

Amen to that. "That's why it's hard for me to believe he had anything to do with Charlene's murder. Are you positively sure you saw Ben carrying her body?"

Annette's gaze flickered around the room, resting for a long moment on the figurines before she said, "Charlene was a terrible person. Ben hated her."

"You didn't answer my question."

"I told the detectives that I *thought* it was Ben, but I might have been mistaken."

A cleverly ambiguous statement. She'd given enough of a hint to point suspicion toward Ben while allowing herself deniability. Was Annette that savvy? It occurred to Liz that someone else might have told her what to say.

Liz stood. "I should go downstairs and give my statement to the CBI. Thanks for talking to me."

Annette played with her long braid. "You're not as bad as I thought you were."

"Back at you."

On her way out, Liz studied the figurines on the dresser. Hiding among them was a flower petal brooch that sparkled with unusual fire. Real diamonds? Real rubies? She picked it up. "This is pretty. It almost looks—"

Annette flew across the room and snatched the shimmering piece of jewelry. "Get out. Now."

Chapter Twelve

Standing in the kitchen with a mug of decaf coffee that Rachel had brewed, Ben apprised Patrice and Monte of the current threat situation. His voice stayed calm. His account was as simple and direct as possible. Carefully, he analyzed Patrice's reactions, hoping that his sister wasn't responsible for the dead elk and the sniper, hoping that she wasn't trying to kill him.

"The road isn't technically our property," she said. "It's maintained by the county. So we really can't prosecute for poaching."

"Damn the elk," he said. "This was attempted murder."

"Oh, Ben. Don't be so dramatic."

She raised the coffee mug to her lips. In her black pajamas, she resembled a high-fashion ninja. With her hair still damp from the shower, she didn't look like she'd been running through the forest.

On the other hand, Monte had on black jeans and a cashmere sweater. Ben didn't really think there was time for him to race back to the house. But he could be wrong.

"Someone tried to kill me," Ben said.

"Are you quite certain?" Her eyebrows raised. "Is your Mustang riddled with bullets?"

"Why would I make this up?"

"It's so very obvious." She exchanged a glance with Monte, who sat at the kitchen table and reached for the plate of cookies that Rachel had laid out. In his other hand, he held a cell phone, which he was using to send text messages.

"Why so obvious?"

"You're trying to divert suspicion from yourself. You probably want to make it look like somebody else killed Charlene."

"I don't need a diversion." He struggled to maintain control. His sister had always been able to poke at his last nerve. "I'm innocent."

Liz joined them in the kitchen, carrying her yellow legal pad. As she poured herself a cup of coffee, she said, "I was in the car with Ben. I witnessed the assault."

"Oh?" Patrice's mouth formed a tight little circle. "And why should I believe Ben's new girlfriend?"

"I'm not his girlfriend."

"Then why are you here? You're totally incompetent as a maid."

"Personal assistant," she said. "I'm here to help Ben handle all the details of running the Crawford family business. And, maybe, to help him solve the murder."

"That's right," he said. "She's working for me."

It had never been his intention to use Liz as his assistant. He hadn't gone to her apartment and begged her to return because he thought she'd make a good employee. On the other hand, she was smart, steady and believed in his innocence. With her as a personal assistant, he might pull out of this mess without being charged for murder.

"Quite the promotion," Patrice snapped. "I hope he's paying you well."

"He is." Liz snapped back. "And I'm worth it."

"Perhaps you two geniuses will enlighten me about this supposed sniper. Why would anyone want to kill Ben?"

Liz responded. "The will."

Patrice pulled back. Her confidence ebbed. "What do you know about the will? Are you familiar with the terms?"

"Are you?" Ben asked.

The corners of her mouth tightened. Ever since she was a little girl, that expression had meant she was lying. Further evidence of her uneasiness came when she reached for a cookie. Patrice never ate after dinner.

"I know nothing," she said.

Monte leaned toward her and held out the screen of his cell phone so she could see. "That's a good offer."

She shook her head. "We can do better."

"What the hell are you doing?" Ben demanded.

Monte cradled the cell phone against his sweater. "We're contacting agents who can sell our personal account of the murder. Maybe a book deal. Or a movie of the week."

"Certainly not the tabloids," Patrice added.

Liz laughed out loud. "Yeah, those tabloids are so low class."

"But they pay well," Monte said. "One of them contacted us right after Patrice read that statement to the media. She looks good on television. The camera loves her. She could do talk shows."

"Oh, good," Ben muttered. "That's just swell."

"Why shouldn't I do *Oprah*?" she demanded. "You're just angry because I'm getting the attention."

"Damn it, Patrice. You picked a hell of a time for sibling rivalry."

He'd been disappointed in his sister many times, but never like this. Patrice had been offered dozens of legitimate opportunities to work in the family business. She could have staked out her own career path. But she never wanted to learn the ropes, couldn't be bothered with details.

Now she was choosing to make her fortune through notoriety. Tabloids. Talk shows. Selling the family history to the highest bidder.

Ben grabbed the plate of cookies and headed toward the door. "You might want to put on a fresh coat of lipstick, Patrice. Agent Lattimer will be here momentarily."

He and Liz went to the study, and he closed the door behind them. Still steamed, he set down his coffee on the table and shoved a cookie into his mouth. How could he and Patrice have come from the same gene pool? "She didn't even ask if I was okay after I told her about the sniper. Hasn't once inquired after Jerod's health."

"Go easy on her," Liz said. "Jerod told me—when he thought I was Charlene—that your sister had a rough time after your parents died."

"She's an adult now. There's only so long you can blame the tragedies of the past."

"Then let's stick to the present. It seemed to me that Patrice was lying when she said she didn't know the terms of the will."

"She probably got Tony to fill her in on the details."

"But I don't think she wants to kill you."

"Not with a sniper's bullet. More likely, she'll tear me

apart, one slow piece at a time, and feed me into the gossip mill."

"Have you got a lot of deep, dark secrets?"

"Nothing I'm ashamed of. Sure, I've had my share of disasters. And then, there's my failed marriage." He cringed inwardly, thinking of how Victoria had played him for a fool. It wasn't the kind of story he wanted to see in a tabloid headline. "I don't like to air my dirty laundry in public."

"I get it. You're more of a private person."

She perched on the edge of his desk with her feet dangling. Her running shoes seemed adorably small, almost dainty. She'd changed out of the red blouse into a long-sleeved brown T-shirt that hid her curves, but she still looked cute. "And you? Now you're my personal assistant?"

"Seemed appropriate," she said without apology.

"And you don't have to wear a maid uniform."

"Bonus."

Her grin went a long way toward defusing his anger. "Bringing you on board might be the best hire I've ever made."

"We've got a ton of stuff to sort out. Number one is hiring a bodyguard."

"I'd rather not."

"A sniper tried to kill you, Ben. And there's a good chance that he's a professional hitman."

He had come to the same conclusion but was interested in hearing her reasoning. "Why do you think he's a pro?"

"Unless there's been an outbreak of homicidal mania, there's only one murderer. The person who killed Charlene is responsible for the attack on you."

"Which brings us back to our list of suspects."

Liz consulted her legal pad and read off the names. "Patrice and Monte. Tony Lansing. Ramon. And Victoria."

"A vile woman," he muttered.

"That's a bit harsh."

Vile was a mild description compared to what he thought of his almost ex-wife. As far as he could tell, the only decent thing she'd ever done was give birth to Natalie. She'd betrayed him with other lovers and robbed him blind. She was greedy, grasping. Vicious. A pit viper. A venomous She-Beast From Hell. "Don't get me started."

"Somehow, I don't see any of these people getting their hands dirty by dragging a dead elk across the road. But they all have enough money to hire a hitman."

"Good point."

"And you have the dough to pay for security."

"You're right."

Especially since Natalie was scheduled to visit on the weekend. He needed to make sure the estate was safe. He rattled off the name of a company he'd used before, and Liz made a note.

Looking down at her legal pad, she frowned. "This list of suspects is kind of skimpy. Who are we forgetting?"

"All of Charlene's friends who were at the party. There could be a lot of grudges we're not aware of."

She scribbled down a note. "Who else? Don't worry about motive, just give me all the names you can think of. Anybody who was in contact with Charlene."

Sipping his coffee, he tried to remember, to think of all the possibilities.

Setting up their own investigation—parallel to the CBI inquiry—wasn't really much different from running a business. Every detail needed to be considered.

"There's the staff, of course. And Jerod's rotating nurses. Hell, I don't even remember the names of most of them, but they might have known Charlene. And Dr. Mancini."

"How long has he been associated with your family?"

"Twenty years. But he's only been a friend of the family for half that long. He started making regular house calls when my grandmother was ill."

"He told Annette that she could be a good nurse."

As he thought of quiet, little Annette, he frowned. She was another woman who meant to do him wrong. "How did she ever come up with that story about me carrying Charlene's body?"

"Because she's desperate for you to notice her. Annette has a major crush on you."

"She has a strange way of showing affection. Accusing me of murder."

"Nonetheless," Liz said. "I talked to her in her room. Have you ever seen that room? It's a junior high school girl's fantasy land. She thinks she's a princess. And you're Prince Charming."

"Great."

She hopped off the desk and pounced on a cookie. "There might be another reason she came up with that story about the monster carrying Charlene. Among Annette's parade of figurines, there was a flower-shaped brooch. I'm no expert, but it looked like real diamonds and a ruby."

"A bribe," he said. "The killer paid her to tell that story."

"Or she saw who it really was, and he's paying her to keep her mouth shut."

If that were the case, Annette was in danger. "I need to talk with her."

"When you do," Liz said, "be gentle."

There was only one woman he wanted to be gentle with. Gentle and tender. That woman was Liz.

Chapter Thirteen

It was after midnight when Liz finally dived between the sheets on the single bed in her garret bedroom. In her plaid jammie bottoms and mismatched polka-dot nightshirt, she wriggled around, trying to find the most comfortable position. Not that it mattered. She was tired enough to sleep standing up. Tired...and oddly happy.

Finally, she knew what it was like to be taken seriously. For most of her life, she'd been a scruffy little blonde, easily ignored. The exception was Dragon Lou's karate school, where her black belt gave her immediate status. In regular life, she was just one of the herd.

As part of the Crawford estate—Ben Crawford's right-hand woman—she got noticed. The CBI agent in charge—Lattimer—had given her a measure of respect when he'd taken her statement. He'd included her when he and Ben had inspected the Mustang, which was unmarked by bullets. Bits of hair from the elk had caught in the wheel wells, but otherwise the car was fine.

The forensic team had gone to investigate the site where the shooting had taken place, but tomorrow the CBI would return. Lattimer had promised an update on their investigation.

Rolling onto her back, Liz considered questions she should ask Agent Lattimer. Results of the autopsy? Alibis for other suspects? She really couldn't believe that the cops were being so cooperative; they liked to play it close to the vest. But Ben had connections that probably went as high as the governor. Whether or not he was a suspect, everybody—including Lattimer—treated him with deference. Wealth had its privileges.

She closed her eyes, knowing that she ought to sleep, but her mind still raced.

She enjoyed being a *real* detective, looking for a murderer, considering motives, seeking out clues. Investigation stimulated her brain. It was way more fun than her dry, repetitive studies in law school. Maybe she ought to consider a change in career.

Stop thinking. Go to sleep.

Or maybe she should sign on permanently as Ben's personal assistant. Remembering the expression on his face when she'd announced her new job made her chuckle. She enjoyed throwing him off guard, shaking up his CEO composure.

As she allowed herself to think of Ben, a whole different part of her anatomy was stimulated. Sometimes, when she looked at him, she felt an electric thrill that started in the pit of her belly and spread to every part of her. And when he touched her? The sexual magnetism between them was growing more intense, harder to resist.

Everyone in the household seemed to think she was sleeping with him. Maybe she should fulfill their expectations.

She heard a sound from the hallway. As if something scratched against her door. Was someone out there?

Listening intently, she heard a faint rustling.

In normal circumstances, she'd roll over and go to sleep. But nothing about this house was normal. The murderer could be lurking in the hall. Her rosy contentment turned a few shades darker. Nothing like a threat to bring a person back to reality.

Liz slipped from the bed and went to her door. Carefully, she turned the knob and peered out into the dimly lit hallway. She heard footsteps on the staircase. Slipping on her moccasins, she followed.

The person on the stairs made no effort to be quiet. Liz matched her footsteps to the sound of theirs, descending at the same pace. In the stairwell off the kitchen, she caught a glimpse of a long flannel nightgown. Annette was wandering again.

Liz stayed in the shadows and watched while Annette bustled around the kitchen, humming to herself. She hadn't turned on the overhead lights; the glow of moonlight through the windows provided enough illumination. She opened cupboards and drawers. What was she doing?

This woman seemed to have a bizarre fantasy life. During the day, she performed her maid duties with silent, invisible efficiency. At night, she took on a different identity. Her humming was interrupted by whispered snatches of conversation. A couple of times, Liz heard her speak Ben's name.

Using the heirloom china and crystal wineglasses, Annette flitted back and forth between kitchen and dining room, laying out two formal place settings at the table—one at each end. She was so caught up in her activity that she didn't notice Liz as she moved through the hallway to get a better view of the dining room.

With the place settings completed, Annette gave a satisfied smile. Holding the folds of her nightgown between her thumb and forefinger as if the fabric were rich silk instead of flannel, she ceremoniously sat at the head of the table. Beaming a smile at her nonexistent guests, she raised her wineglass. Her movements were studied and graceful. In the reflected moonlight from the windows, the oval of her face shone with a feverish radiance.

Her lips moved, but Liz couldn't decipher the words. Sad, lonely Annette was completely consumed in her alternate reality. She wanted this lifestyle so much, with such fierce desperation, that she was compelled to act out her dream of being a princess.

As Liz watched, sympathy welled up inside her. She'd known plenty of other women—including her own mother—who had given up their self-respect in search of an improbable dream. Annette's midnight performance was heartbreaking.

She reached into the pocket of her nightgown and took out the diamond brooch, which she fastened at her throat.

Her mood changed. She covered her eyes with her hands. Sobs shook her shoulders.

Liz wondered if she should step out of the shadows and offer comfort, but she feared that making her presence known might snap Annette's tenuous grasp on reality.

"Damn you all," Annette shouted as she bolted to her feet. "You can go to hell. Especially you, Ben."

She fled from the table and darted toward the stairwell.

A chill crawled up Liz's legs, and she hugged her arms around her waist. Though she still had sympathy for Annette, there was some serious craziness going on in that woman. She could be dangerous.

From the front staircase, she heard someone approaching. The dining room light snapped on. Ben stood there in jeans and a T-shirt. "Liz?"

"Hi there." Her voice was shaky.

He gestured to the place settings. "What are you doing?"

She peeked over her shoulder toward the kitchen, hoping that Annette had fled to her room and locked the door. Telling him the truth seemed like a betrayal.

He asked, "Why is the good china on the table?"

"Annette was wandering again. I heard a noise outside my room and followed her down here, where she laid out these place settings." She paused. This was where the explanation got weird. "It looked like she was having some kind of imaginary dinner party."

"I don't get it."

She picked up one of the plates. "Let's put this stuff away."

"Seriously, Liz. I don't understand what you're saying about Annette."

When he started to stack the salad plates and the saucers, she stopped him. "Take them one by one. Rachel told me we have to be mega-careful with the expensive heirlooms."

"And we don't want Rachel on our ass." He carried one plate in each hand and followed her into the kitchen. "Annette's delusional wanderings in the middle of the night are too much. She's got to go."

"You're going to fire her?"

"First thing tomorrow."

With a quick pivot, Liz marched back into the dining room for another couple of plates. She didn't want Annette to be fired. Certainly not because of something she said.

In the kitchen, she whirled and faced him. "Firing her is an overreaction. Annette was only playing a game.

Kind of like a little girl having a tea party with her dolls. She's harmless."

"She's crazy."

"What if this was an illness? Obviously, Annette has insomnia. That might lead to sleepwalking."

"I'm not running a psychiatric clinic. I don't have time for Annette's delusional behavior."

"Everybody has fantasies." She tried to think of a comparison he could relate to. "Think of sports. Haven't you ever dreamed about being on the PGA tour? Or throwing the winning touchdown in the Super Bowl and having the crowd go wild?" She leaned toward him. This was the clincher. "How about winning the America's Cup? Huh? Ever imagine that?"

"It's not the same thing." He placed two salad bowls on the counter. "How the hell could anybody fantasize about eating dinner?"

"Having dinner served to her. Using the fancy china. Wearing fabulous jewelry." She touched the neck of her T-shirt, indicating where Annette had fastened the brooch on her own neck. "She has this desperate longing to be a fairy princess. To sit at the dinner table with you. Prince Charming."

"Fine. Her next job can be at Disneyland."

The gulf between them had never gaped so widely. He had all the power, the status, the prestige. He was the boss. People like her and Annette were nothing but employees—functionaries whose sole purpose was to make his life easier.

Earlier, when she had gone to bed, Liz had been pleased with herself. And with him. Now she could barely stand to look at his annoyingly handsome face. Some phony Prince Charming he turned out to be. His arrogance picked apart the last of her good mood. And she was angry.

Blushing again. This time from rage and deep-seeded resentment. She remembered every time she'd lost a job or been chastised by an idiot supervisor.

"Why would I expect you to understand?" She glared at him. "You don't know what it's like to struggle. You've always been rich."

"I've worked every job in the Crawford businesses. I started as a roughneck in the oil fields."

"But that was just a field trip for you. Any time you wanted, you could return to luxury. You could have your gourmet chef prepare your dinners. Have your butler brush lint off the shoulder of your two-thousand-dollar jacket."

"I'm not like that."

"But you are." She picked up one of the plates. "You eat off heirloom china."

"That's enough."

His tone was clipped and harsh. His jaw clenched as his anger rose up to match her own. Now would have been the smart time to back down, but her fuse had been lit. She was on her way to total explosion.

"What's the matter, Ben? Not used to being talked back to by one of your underlings?"

"Give it a rest, Liz. I want you to stop. Now."

"Don't tell me what to do." She kept her voice low. Other people were sleeping. "I might be your employee, but you don't own me."

"And you don't know me." He took a step closer to her. The heat of his anger washed toward her. "I don't give a damn about money or the things that money can buy. Like this plate."

He picked it up and prepared to hurl it to the floor. She grasped his arm. "Don't."

"Why not? It doesn't matter to me."

"Just don't," she said.

"Because you're concerned about the cost. Right? You're the one who puts too much value on things. You. Not me."

"Break all the plates you want," she said. "But not in here. You'll wake everybody up."

Without another word, he gathered up the two place settings, stacking them carelessly. He hooked his fingers through the teacups, grabbed the wineglasses. In a few strides, he was at the back door.

Now what? She followed as he stormed out into the night. "You shouldn't be out here. The sniper could still be around."

He circled to the left of the house onto a path that led through the trees. Moonlight cast blue-gray shadows at the edges of towering pines and leafy shrubs. As she ran to keep up with Ben's long-legged stride, she stumbled. The thin soles of her moccasins provided little protection from the rocks and twigs, but she wasn't about to turn back. She had to see this through.

Finally, he stopped in a small clearing. They were out of sight from the house, separated by a wall of pine trees. Squatting down, he placed the delicate china on a bed of pine needles. Then he stood.

Breathing hard from running, she stared at him. In his jeans and T-shirt, he looked like he belonged in this rugged setting. The mountains gave him a stature he would never achieve from a bank account. He looked strong, tall and aggressively masculine. Who was this guy? A hard-driving CEO? A cowboy? A sea captain?

"You're right," she said. "I don't really know you."

"Know this," he said. "Everything I do, every decision I make, is to serve those I love."

"Firing Annette?"

"Day after tomorrow, Natalie will be staying here for three days. I don't want my daughter to be frightened by Annette's delusional fantasies."

Liz hadn't considered what it would be like to have a child on the premises. "This isn't a good time for Natalie to visit. Not with the murder investigation. And a sniper. And Jerod being in the hospital."

"I'll protect her. And Jerod." He picked up one of the salad plates. "And you."

"Me?"

With a flick of his wrist, he flipped the plate like a Frisbee. The edge hit a flat granite boulder. The sound of breaking china echoed in the forest. Ben laughed. "Oh, yeah. That feels good."

She edged closer. "What do you mean when you say you'll protect me?"

He grabbed another plate, hefted its weight in his hands. "I want your trust, Liz. You believed in my innocence when everybody else was ready to condemn me, but you still think I'm some kind of spoiled preppy jerk. I want you to believe in me the way I believe in you."

His words struck her very soul. She'd come to the Crawford estate to find evidence to use against him. She didn't deserve his trust.

He fired another plate against the rock, grinned and said, "If I have to smash every heirloom in the house to prove that money doesn't matter to me, I'll do it."

"You have a strange way of proving your point."

He dangled a fancy teacup from his finger. "This is a hell of a lot more fun than arguing."

The problem wasn't him. It was her. She'd been lying from the first moment they'd met. She'd hidden behind her working class morality. Her assumption that rich people—like Ben—wanted only to take advantage of others was dead wrong. He was a good man.

Moving toward him, she held out her hand. "Give me one of those priceless bowls."

She flung it hard. The sound of shattering china gave her a thrill. "Nice," she said. "Kind of liberating."

"You think?" He threw a crystal goblet. The shards sparkled like diamonds in the moonlight. "I say, the hell with fancy place settings."

"And maids in uniforms."

"And ten-course dinners."

Clearly, they were both behaving badly. Out of control. Wild and crazy. She loved it.

Grabbing the last dinner plate, she lifted it over her head with both hands and threw. Never again would a maid have to carry this delicate piece into the kitchen and carefully store it away.

When they were down to the last saucer, he held it toward her. "Go ahead."

"You take the shot." In a parody of manners, she added, "I insist."

He pressed the saucer into her grasp. She looked up into his face. The night breeze stroked his brown hair. The gleam from a thousand stars outlined the sinews in his muscular arms.

She glided her fingertips along his forearm and felt a slight quiver beneath his skin. The night air between them shimmered, and the glow drew her toward him. She would no longer resist their magnetism. Her arms slipped around him. The saucer fell to the ground, unbroken.

He yanked her tightly against him. His kiss was fierce and demanding. Her body responded with a burst of pent-up passion. All restraint vanished as she threw herself into that long, delicious kiss.

Her breasts flattened against the hard muscles of his chest. She rubbed herself against his erection. His excitement fed her own desire.

Ending the kiss, he drew back, giving her the space to say no. His eyes were fiery sapphires. His lips, drawn back from his straight white teeth, beckoned to her. She wanted him. All of him.

"Yes," she whispered.

Still not kissing her, his gaze heated her skin. His hand slipped under her polka-dot nightshirt and ascended her bare midriff, finding her breast. His fingers plucked her taut nipple, setting off an incredible electric reaction.

She gasped. Her head rolled back, and he nibbled the line of her throat. Tingles shot through her. *Amazing. Fantastic.*

She wasn't sure how they ended up on the ground, but she was definitely prone. And he rose above her on his elbows. His legs spread to straddle her hips.

Arching her back, she writhed against him. She shoved aside the fabric of his shirt and stroked his chest. She wanted more. Her arms pulled him closer. She wanted his full weight pressed against her.

"Liz," he whispered her name.

"Yes, Ben. I already said yes."

"I don't have a condom."

The pressure inside her deflated. Oh, yes, she wanted to make love. But she wasn't about to take the risk of unprotected sex. "Couldn't we ring for a servant to bring one?"

"A condom valet?"

He fell to the ground beside her. They lay side-by-side, panting as they looked up through a tracery of pine boughs to the starry skies. Leftover tremors of anticipation trembled through her.

Maybe they could take this passion inside to his bedroom—make love like normal people in an actual bed. But she wasn't ready for premeditated sex. Too many other issues stood between them.

And the moment had passed.

Chapter Fourteen

Ben started early the next morning. By eight o'clock, he was showered, shaved and dressed in jeans and a blue workshirt with the sleeves rolled up. He grabbed a cup of coffee in the kitchen and went directly into the study, where he was pleasantly surprised to find Liz sitting behind the desk.

In deference to her new position as his personal assistant, she'd taken more care with her wardrobe. Her scoop neck, short-sleeved T-shirt actually fit. The bright blue fabric outlined her breasts and slender waist very nicely. When she stood, he saw she was wearing gray pinstriped trousers.

He focused on her feet. Her pink toes were visible in dressy, black sandals. "You're wearing heels."

"Hey, I'm a girl." She posed like a model. "It's my power suit. I had to get something appropriate for mock court, and this is it."

"Very powerful." And very sexy.

Given the slightest encouragement, he was ready to throw her across the desk and take her right here. But Liz was all business. She returned to the desk chair and gestured to the computer screen. "You've got lots of e-mails. Several from Crawford Aero-Equipment in Seattle and some from Charlene's friends. Oh, and—"

"Hold it. How did you get into my e-mail?"

"It didn't take a genius to figure out that your password was *Natalie*."

"You might be too smart for your own good."

"There's no such thing as too smart." She stood and re-linquished the swivel chair behind the desk. "Before we get into the e-mail, you've had some important phone calls. One was from Agent Lattimer. He'll be here in about an hour to update you on the CBI investigation. The other was from Jerod's doctor."

Apprehension tightened his throat. He forced himself to swallow a sip of coffee. "Did the doc sound positive?"

She nodded. "He wants to operate today."

Sinking into the chair behind his desk, Ben replayed the advice he'd heard from the specialists and neurosurgeons. There was risk in operating. His grandpa was seventy-six years old, and his health had been compromised by the tumor in his brain. He'd lost weight and motor skills. His vision was nearly gone. However, if they didn't operate, Jerod would surely be dead before the end of the year. "It's his decision."

"He wants to be well," she said. "When he's talked to me—thinking I'm Charlene—he's told me how much he wants to be strong again. To see the sunlight shimmering on the lake. He's tired of being sick."

He picked up the phone from its cradle. "We'll head down to the hospital right after we talk to Lattimer."

The hour passed quickly and smoothly. With Liz helping him organize and holding the rest of his demanding household at bay, Ben glided through the workload. His only real stumbling block was coming up with an obituary for Charlene. She had two ex-husbands but no other family that he knew of. No children. She'd been involved in a couple of charities, but he wasn't sure which ones.

When Agent Lattimer entered the study, his attitude was more like a business executive than a cop. His beige suit fit well, and his loafers were polished.

After shaking hands, he took a seat on the sofa and flipped open a small spiral notebook. "I'm afraid we didn't find much evidence from your sniper attack last night. There was a spot on the hillside that he might have used. The sightline to the elk was excellent."

"What about footprints?" Liz asked.

"Nothing but smudges. The soil is too rocky."

"How about bullets or casings?"

Lattimer shook his head. "He cleaned up."

"A professional," Ben said.

"We're the professionals." Lattimer looked down at his notes. "The CBI forensics teams are second to none. Highly trained. Highly efficient. And we found nothing. If Liz hadn't been along as a witness, I might not believe there was a sniper."

Ben was taken aback. So much for the sniper attack's removing him from top spot as a suspect in Charlene's murder.

"But there was a bullet," Liz said. "In the elk."

"From a 12-gauge shotgun. Nothing remarkable. No indication of the silencer you claim he used."

Claim? As if he were making this up? Ben folded his arms across his chest and grumbled. Apparently, he had to be shot and bleeding to prove his innocence.

Liz was handling Lattimer with far more finesse. She poured fresh coffee from a thermal carafe and offered him fresh rhubarb muffins baked this morning by the chef. Her smile was sweeter than honey. "Can you give us an update on your murder investigation?"

"There's not much to tell." Lattimer helped himself to a muffin and peeled away the wrapper. "Our forensics are inconclusive. In the log barn—the crime scene—we found a number of fingerprints, including yours, Ben."

"It's my workshop." Being surly would get him nowhere, but he couldn't help being frustrated. "Of course my prints are there."

"What about on the murder weapon?" Liz asked.

"Wiped clean," the agent responded. "Tell me again, Liz. What's your interest in this investigation?"

"I'm Ben's personal assistant."

"The first time we talked, you were wearing a maid's uniform."

"Big promotion," she said with another big smile. She was positively oozing hospitality. "What about footprints? Fibers?"

"We have dozens of footprints—shoes, boots and barefoot—going up and down the hillside. Nothing to clearly indicate the murderer."

Liz continued to ask the questions. "You mentioned that the barn is the murder scene. Was she killed there?"

"Yes."

"So," Ben said, "when Annette said she saw someone carrying Charlene's lifeless body, she was mistaken."

"Not necessarily," Liz contradicted him. "Charlene could have been drugged and then carried. Is that what happened, Agent Lattimer? Do you have autopsy results?"

Lattimer shifted uncomfortably on the sofa but still managed to take a giant bite of the muffin. "It's highly

unorthodox for me to share this information. I hope
you're aware of that, Mr. Crawford."

"I appreciate your cooperation," Ben said. He didn't
need to remind the agent of his many highly placed po-
litical friends who wanted to keep Ben as a happy
campaign contributor. "About the autopsy?"

"Charlene was drugged. Nothing lethal. A sedative
combined with the alcohol in her system to knock her
out."

"How about witnesses?" Ben said. "I assume you've
spoken to the other people at the party. Did they notice
Charlene stumbling around?"

He finished off his muffin and washed it down with a
swig of coffee. "I can't talk to you about the testimony
or alibis of other witnesses, except to say that no one at
the party noticed anything unusual when they went
upstairs to bed."

"Ramon left early," Liz said. "Did anyone see him
go?"

Lattimer stood. "That's really all I can say right now.
If I have a significant break in the case, you'll be
informed."

After they showed Lattimer to the door, Ben turned to
face the chaos that had already developed this morning.

The first face he saw was Rachel's, her eyebrows
pulled down in a ferocious scowl. "Sir," she whispered,
"something terrible has happened."

More terrible than murder? Than a sniper attack? Than
being suspected of a major crime? "What?"

"Two settings of the good china are missing." She cast
dark glances to the left and right. "Someone must have
stolen them."

"I took the place settings."

Her mouth flopped open and closed a couple of times like a fish out of water. "You, sir?"

"Is there anything else? I need to see Jerod at the hospital."

"Tony Lansing arrived a few moments ago. He's in the dining room. And there's a gentleman from a security company. He said you called him about bodyguards."

Tony could wait. "Where's the security guy?"

"Front room."

He strode forward, intending to make quick work of these issues and get to the hospital. "Come with me, Rachel. I'll need your assistance."

After a firm handshake with the security guy, whose neck was bigger than Liz's waist, Ben said he wanted full protection at the estate, including someone to monitor the front gate and keep the reporters under control.

"Also," Liz interrupted, "you need a personal body-guard to accompany you when you drive in and out of Denver."

"How many men?" the security guy asked.

"As many as necessary," Ben said. "And as soon as possible. Rachel will give you the identifications for people who work here. Thank you."

Now for Tony Lansing. Ben stalked across the foyer with Liz at his heels. "That was fast," she said.

"I'm a decisive guy."

And there wasn't time for dancing around. He needed things taken care of. In the dining room, Ben didn't bother shaking hands. He circled the table and leaned down to stare Tony straight in the eye. "You want to be the Crawford family attorney, right?"

"Yeah." He struggled to keep his gaze steady.

"Here's your first assignment. I want you here. All

day. Don't let anybody—namely Patrice—do anything stupid. Do not talk to the press."

"You can count on me."

That remained to be seen. "And I want you to put together an obituary for Charlene. Find out when the body will be released and make funeral arrangements."

Again, Tony nodded. He seemed relieved he wasn't being asked to do anything difficult or outrageous, and Ben allowed him to think he was safe until he got to the door leading out of the dining room. Then he turned, "One more thing, Tony."

"What's that?"

"I want a copy of Jerod's new will. And Charlene's."

"Interesting that you mention Charlene's will. I need to do an inventory of her things. Technically, I can't release either of those documents to you without—"

"Make it happen," Ben said.

He caught a glimpse of Annette, who immediately dashed off in the opposite direction. Though he still intended to fire her delusional little self, it would have to wait. He and Liz had almost made it to the front door when Patrice caught up with him. "Where are you going? What are you doing? I have a terrible headache."

"Deal with it," he said.

"I mean it, Ben. My head is killing me. I need something more than aspirin."

"Call Dr. Mancini." The family doctor had been coming here daily for months, might as well pay for one more house call. "I'm going to the hospital, Patrice. The doctors are probably going to operate on Jerod today."

For a moment, he saw a flicker of concern in her eyes. He hoped that—for once in her selfish life—she might be thinking of someone else. Might be worrying about her grandpa, the man who had made her expensive lifestyle possible, the man who had always cared for her.

Just as quickly, her compassion disappeared. She frowned. "Are you leaving me here alone?"

"Tony's here. And a team of bodyguards. You'll be okay."

He hoped he could say the same for Jerod.

ALONE AT A SQUARE TABLE IN THE hospital cafeteria, Liz stared into the depths of her coffee cup and worried. Hospitals always made her nervous. It should have been the other way around; this was a place people came for healing and hope. She desperately wanted to believe that Jerod would recover.

She'd stuck by Ben's side while he'd talked with the two specialists and the brain surgeon. They'd reviewed the results from Jerod's tests; most of what they'd said about micro-lasers and neuro-systems stretched far beyond her comprehension. She wished the doctors would have given odds on the operation, like one in three. Or a percentage—ninety percent sure he'll make it. But neurosurgery wasn't roulette. All they'd say was that Jerod's heart was strong and the tumor appeared to be operable.

One of the specialists had made a point of complimenting Ben on providing the experimental treatment his grandpa had needed. Whatever that meant. She'd ask him later.

Jerod's recovery stayed foremost in her mind, but she had plenty of concerns about Ben. Constant activity swirled around him like a sucking whirlpool. There was the long-distance running of his business in Seattle. And keeping the Crawford estate operational. And the custody battle over his daughter. And Charlene's murder.

Most of all, the murder. Though Agent Lattimer had been respectful, his suspicions still centered on Ben, who had plenty of motive and ample opportunity to slip a sedative into Charlene's drink.

If she and Ben didn't concentrate on solving the murder, he might end up in jail.

Then, there was the sniper. Though the personal body-guard had shown up at the hospital and was—at this very moment—watching Ben's back, the threat remained.

With a sigh, she swizzled her spoon through the coffee. Apparently, it would be her job to think about Ben's safety and to prove his innocence. And, last but not least, to lift his burden of concern about Jerod.

There was one person Liz could always turn to in times of trouble and frustration. She left the table and went outside to use her cell phone.

He answered on the first ring. "Schooner Detective Agency."

"Harry, I need you." She gave him the address of the hospital. "And bring your gun."

Chapter Fifteen

An hour before the operation, Jerod seemed to be in good spirits. Ben stood beside his grandpa's bed, watching as Liz in her platinum wig gave a strange yet credible performance as Charlene, doused in her signature perfume. Liz modified her gestures to a flutter. Her voice was pitched higher than her normal tone, and she made a conscious effort to start every sentence with *I*.

Exactly right. Vanity had been the essence of Charlene. Self-centered to the core. Flighty and thoughtless. Demanding and…pretty damned funny on occasion. He would miss her foot-stamping, hair-tossing arguments.

What if she'd been right to keep Jerod away from the surgeons? What if the operation failed?

His grandpa scowled in Ben's direction. "How come you're so quiet, boy?"

"Thinking." And worrying.

"I'm fixing to do a whole lot of cogitating after I get my brain tuned up. Maybe take up some kind of hobby."

"You used to play guitar," Ben said.

He'd never forget those days. Long ago when his family had been whole and happy, Grandpa Jerod would haul his twelve-string out onto the front porch of the

Texas house after dinner. With daylight fading into night, he'd strum by himself for a bit. Then everybody would gather around to sing cowboy love songs about Clementine and Suzannah. Little Patrice would twirl in time to the music. His parents would sit side-by-side on the porch swing with his mother's head resting on his father's shoulder. His grandma would always sing soprano in a high, clear voice.

Ben missed those family nights. He missed his grandma. His mom. His dad. Damn it, he couldn't bear to lose Jerod, too.

"Sing for me," Liz said. "Come on, bumblebee. One little tune."

"You've never much cared for my singing, honey. I believe you referred to my voice as a rusty hinge."

"A girl can change her mind," Liz said, giving a toss of her platinum wig.

Jerod cleared his throat and rumbled, "Do not forsake me…"

Liz joined in. "Oh, my darlin'."

Ben would have added his baritone to the chorus, but he didn't trust himself to sing without betraying the strong emotions that roiled inside him. His abiding grief. His love for Jerod. His fear about this surgery.

When the song ended, Liz gave Jerod a hug. "Listen up," she said to him. "I have a friend I want you to meet."

"Hell's bells, Charlene. Now's not the time for me to be saying howdy to one of your pretty little pals."

"You'll like this guy," she said confidently. "He's going to stay right here at the hospital and make sure everything goes okay."

He grumbled, "I don't need a babysitter."

"Please, bumblebee. For me. Plee-eeze."

Liz's exaggerated pout—just right for Charlene but so out of character for her—lightened Ben's mood. The pain was still there, but she made it bearable.

When she'd told him her plan to have a friend of hers stay with his grandpa, he'd approved. Jerod's operation could take several hours, and he'd be unconscious in recovery for hours after that. Though Ben had hoped to stay at the hospital, too many other things were happening. Last time he'd checked his cell phone, there had been three urgent text messages from Tony Lansing.

"Oh, look," Liz bubbled. "My friend is here already. Jerod Crawford, I want you to meet Harry Schooner."

Though Liz had told him that Harry was older, Ben expected someone in his forties. Upon meeting this white-haired, heavyset, rumpled man, he added twenty years to his estimate. According to Liz, Harry had once been a cop, and he had the world-weary look of someone who had seen it all. The bulge under his plaid jacket also indicated that he was wearing a shoulder holster.

As Harry shook Jerod's hand, he asked, "How's the food in this joint?"

"Not bad if you're partial to green Jell-O."

"I might have to smuggle in a couple of steaks. You're from Texas," Harry said. "You know beef."

"Damn right, I do." Jerod sat up a bit straighter.

"I'll leave you two to get acquainted," Liz said. "Ben and I need to step out in the hall for a moment."

He joined her in the corridor outside his grandpa's private room. "I like Harry. But why is he wearing a gun?"

"With a homicidal maniac on the loose, it doesn't hurt to have a little extra protection for Jerod."

It didn't surprise him that she was best buddies with

somebody who routinely strapped on a shoulder holster. "What else is on your mind?"

"I checked my cell phone. I have an urgent text message from Tony."

"Me, too." Nothing could possibly be as important as spending these last moments with Jerod before his surgery. "He'll have to wait."

She reached out and took his hands. Though the platinum wig perched atop her head looked vaguely deranged, she was a pillar of sanity. Her green eyes shone with gentle compassion. "How are you holding up?"

"I'm hoping this is the right thing. This surgery."

"It was Jerod's decision to let the doctors operate," she reminded him.

"But he wouldn't be here if it wasn't for me. Or if Charlene were still alive."

She gave his hands a squeeze, and that slight physical contact made him want more. He wanted to wrap himself in her arms and hide from his doubts about Jerod's recovery. He squeezed back and said, "Go ahead and return Tony's call. I'll stay here."

With a wink and a grin, she rushed down the corridor to an area that was okay for cell phones.

When Ben returned to the hospital room, he found Jerod and Harry talking like old buddies. Though they'd only met a moment ago, the two men had shared enough life experiences to make them familiar.

"Tell me about this brain operation," Harry said. "Are they going to shave your head?"

"Ain't going to let them." Jerod raked his gnarled fingers through his thick, white hair. "The doctor said they're going into my brain through my nose."

"Shouldn't be hard. That's a good-sized honker you've got there."

These two were well-matched. It occurred to Ben that his grandpa didn't spend much time with people his own age. Charlene had directed their social life toward a younger crowd. Did he miss his old friends? Was there someone Ben should call?

When Liz came back to the room, she motioned for him to step outside. In a tense whisper, she said, "Lattimer came back to the house with a CBI forensics team. They have a search warrant."

"What are they looking for?"

"Drugs." Her gaze searched his face. "Like the ones they found in Charlene's system."

Trouble. They needed to return to the house as soon as possible. Ben had a few secrets that he would rather not share with law enforcement.

As she and Ben left the hospital, Liz wished she could have matched Jerod's upbeat attitude when the nurses wheeled him off toward the operating room. He'd given a thumbs-up sign and waved. She hadn't been so cheerful as they'd climbed into the back of the SUV driven by Ben's bodyguard—a big, silent hulk of a man who reminded her of the bouncer at the Grizzly Moon, a dance club where beer was free for women on Wednesday nights.

The bodyguard's presence made conversation difficult. She wanted to hug Ben and reassure him, but he had retreated into CEO mode, concentrating entirely on returning phone calls.

When they reached the gates outside the Crawford

estate, they had to drive through a flock of photographers and reporters, some with news trucks and microphones.

Inside the house, they were immediately surrounded. Patrice and Monte. The security guys. Rachel. And Tony Lansing, who was well on his way to being drunk, although it was only noon.

Lattimer and his CBI agents had already departed, but they'd confiscated several items and thrown the already dysfunctional house into chaos.

Liz should have stayed with Ben, should have supported him. But she felt like she was being buried alive under a landslide of stress. Her chest was tight. She needed to breathe.

With a word to him, she slipped away from the crowd and went outside onto the lower deck. Standing at the railing, she looked out on the shimmering lake beneath clear, blue springtime skies. Though she couldn't see the front gate, she heard the distant chatter of dozens of voices. A security guy in a military-type uniform patrolled at the edge of the dock. She should have felt safe, but fear weighed heavily on her mind. Fear for Ben. She knew that he was in possession of illegal drugs; she'd seen him make the buy from the sleazebag dealer in Denver.

Though she hadn't been able to unearth his stash, she suspected that a dedicated team of CBI agents would find it. He'd be in even deeper trouble than he was right now.

Ben stepped up to the banister and joined her. "It's a perfect day for sailing."

"To the ends of the earth," she agreed. Voices from reporters at the gate mingled with the sound of an argument inside the house. "I'd like to be somewhere quiet."

"Sailboats are never silent. There's always the wind

and the lapping of waves." He turned his face to the sun. "Mysterious echoes from the vast blue sea."

The poetic side of his personality captivated her. His brilliant blue eyes gazed into the faraway distance, finding a place where hope thrived and swashbuckling adventure was the order of the day. Easily, she imagined him as the captain of a tallship, standing at the prow with a spyglass held to his eye. Even more easily, she imagined sailing away with him.

Instead, she kept her feet firmly planted on the cedar planks of the lower deck. She asked, "Did Lattimer find anything with his search warrant?"

"He confiscated every pill and capsule in the house, including Patrice's array of Valium and sedatives." He shrugged. "It was a damn good search. Those guys are professional. They even found my drug stash."

Her heart dropped. This was the moment she'd feared. "Your drugs?"

"No big deal. I expect I'll have to pay some kind of fine or something."

How could he be so nonchalant? "You told me that you didn't use drugs."

"I don't." He looked down at her. "This medicine was for Jerod. An experimental drug from Mexico that hasn't been approved by the FDA."

Relief exploded inside her; she felt like singing. "That's what the doctor meant when he mentioned the treatment that you gave Jerod."

"Apparently, the drug helped. It wasn't enough to eradicate the tumor but slowed the growth." He frowned. "You wouldn't believe what I had to go through to get my hands on those pills."

"Oh, yes," she said. "I would."

His late-night visit to the drug dealer made perfect sense. He wasn't a scumbag drug addict; his reason for making an illegal drug buy was heroic. He'd risked his life to help his grandpa.

Unable to hold back, she flung her arms around his neck and kissed him hard on the mouth. Her doubts about his character disappeared.

After returning her kiss, his arms tightened around her. His mouth nuzzled her ear. "I'm not complaining, but what's this all about?"

"You're a good man, Ben."

"Took you long enough to notice."

Though aware that she shouldn't be clinging to him out here in the open where everybody could see them, she didn't let go. Didn't care what other people thought.

Ben was all that mattered.

"We need to find that murderer," she said.

"Damn right."

"You wouldn't look good in an orange prison jumpsuit."

He smiled down at her. "I should get back inside. I want to talk to Tony before he's completely drunk."

She separated from him. "I'll join you in a minute. Downstairs by the bar."

He leaned down to kiss her cheek. "See you then."

After he stepped inside, Liz indulged in a moment of fist-pumping congratulations. *Yes! Yes! Yes!* She'd been right about Ben. He had a perfectly rational reason for consorting with drug dealers. Still not a great idea. But completely understandable.

She couldn't wait to tell Harry.

Liz smacked her fist on the cedar banister, pivoted and strolled toward the sliding glass doors that led into the house.

Hearing a scraping noise over her head, Liz paused. She looked up. One of the long cedar flower boxes shook. Then crashed to the deck.

Chapter Sixteen

Mangled petunia petals and dirt from the splintered flower box scattered at her feet. If Liz had taken one more step forward, she would have been hit. An accident? A coincidence that she'd almost been brained by falling flowers? She thought not.

Someone had loosened the bolts that held that flower box in place, then had given a good hard shove.

She stared at the upper deck and saw no one. But someone had been there only seconds ago, and she intended to find out who it was. She kicked off her heels and ran. At the side of the house, she raced up the wooden staircase that led to the upper level and Jerod's bedroom.

When she flung open the door to the hallway, she saw Rachel with a stack of sheets and towels piled high in her arms. Her eyes widened at the sight of Liz charging toward her. "What's wrong?"

"Did you see anyone come out of Jerod's room?"

"No." She scowled. "His room will be closed off until he comes home from the hospital. I have changed the sheets, of course, and—"

"Stand right here," Liz said. "Don't let anyone come past you."

"Would you please tell me what—"

"No time." Liz returned to the cedar deck that ran along the edge of the upper floor. If she was in luck, the person who'd tried to kill her with a flower box was still in Jerod's room. She could catch them red-handed.

Circling to the deck outside the sliding glass doors, she took a breath and mentally prepared herself to deal with an attacker. Peering through the glass, she saw no one.

When she whipped open the sliding door, a vase of lilies flew past her shoulder and shattered against the wall. What was it with this person and flowers?

Liz dodged forward, moving fast. Annette stood in the middle of the room. Apparently, she'd been hiding behind Jerod's bed. Her arm drew back to throw another object, but Liz shot out with a quick karate chop, disarming her.

Annette yelped in pain.

"Why?" Liz snapped.

"You were kissing him," she said. "I saw you on the lower deck. Kissing Ben."

She rushed forward with arms flailing. This sort of girlish attack was actually more difficult to deal with than someone who knew what they were doing. Liz hesitated, not wanting to do serious damage to Annette, who managed to land one weak blow on her shoulder, then another on her upper arm.

Enough was enough. Liz caught hold of one of those windmilling arms and flipped Annette to the floor. Immediately, she rolled to her stomach and started to sob. "You promised. You swore you weren't sleeping with him."

Liz didn't bother to deny the accusation. She might not be having sex with Ben right now, but his bed was most definitely in her future plans. Not that her love life was any of Annette's business. She looked down at the weepy little maid and would have felt sorry for her if Annette hadn't been so venomous in her lies. "You obviously care about Ben. Why did you make up that story about seeing him carrying Charlene's body?"

"I didn't make it up." Her fist hammered the carpet. "I saw someone and it *might* have been Ben."

"Who was it?"

Her knees pulled up as she curled into a ball, hiding her face. "I don't know."

Annette's craziness had tainted the murder investigation; the CBI agents took her story seriously and focused their suspicions on Ben. "Tell me. Who was it?"

"Don't know."

Liz's patience snapped. She crouched down beside Annette and turned her so she could see into her watery eyes. "When I was in your room, I saw a diamond brooch. Where did you get it?"

"I don't have to tell you."

"Who gave you that pin?"

Her lips pinched together in a stubborn, sour knot.

Disgusted, Liz released her. "You can lie to me, but not to Agent Lattimer. There's a penalty for lying to the police."

"You won't tell him about that pin."

"Goddamn it." Liz seldom used profanity. In her teens, she'd made a conscious decision to avoid gutter talk. Her swearing was a measure of just how angry she was. "I damn well will tell Lattimer about those diamonds. Why are you so scared? Oh, hell. Did you steal the pin?"

She gasped. "It was a gift."

"And who gave it to you?"

"I promised I wouldn't say."

"It's called obstruction of justice," Liz said. "You could go to jail. So you better start telling the truth."

Annette inhaled a shaky breath. "Ramon Stephens gave me the pin. It was right after I saw the monster."

"How soon after?"

"A minute or two."

"So Ramon wasn't the monster?"

Annette shook her head. "He came out on the deck beside me. I was upset, and he tried to comfort me. He said that he'd seen the monster, too. And it looked like Ben."

Liz took a moment to digest this unexpected piece of information. She'd almost written off Ramon, but he was responsible for planting suspicion of Ben in Annette's brain. "Did he give you the pin as payment? For telling the police that Ben was the monster?"

"Nothing like that." Her ingenuousness was too exaggerated to be real. "But I thought he might be right about Ben."

"Why was Ramon carrying a diamond brooch in his pocket?"

"It belonged to Charlene. Jerod gave her all kinds of expensive jewelry that looked like flowers."

"Right." Flowers fit into that whole bumblebee and honey thing. "If you knew the brooch belonged to Charlene, why did you take it?"

"She must have given it to him." Annette's fingers clenched tightly, desperately. "It was his. And he gave it to me. I didn't steal it."

But she knew who the jewelry really belonged to. On some level, Annette must have known that Ramon was using her, getting her to point an accusing finger at Ben.

Liz tried one last time for a positive identification. "Who was it? Who carried Charlene?"

"He had on a hooded sweatshirt. I couldn't tell." Her

lower lip quivered. "What's going to happen to me now? Are you going to tell the CBI?"

Oh, yeah. Liz intended to leave this simpering little witch in the custody of one of the security men to wait for Lattimer.

Ben had been right about firing Annette. Not only was she borderline nuts, but she was also dangerous.

BEN SAT AT THE BAR IN THE downstairs party room beside Tony Lansing, who had managed to perform the task he'd been assigned. His secretary had faxed copies of both Jerod's and Charlene's wills.

For the past twenty minutes, Ben had studied the twelve closely typed pages of his grandpa's new will. The terms were what he expected. The only person who benefited from having Charlene die before his grandfather was his daughter, which also meant her legal guardians. Namely, Victoria and him. "Am I missing something?"

"What you see is what it is." Tony raised a glass of vodka to his mouth and took a healthy swallow. "Unless Jerod changes his mind again, your daughter will be a very wealthy young lady when he passes."

"Why now? Why did he make this change?"

"It's not unusual for someone with a terminal illness. Facing death makes a man think about his loved ones. According to the old will and the prenup, Charlene got five hundred thousand. Jerod wanted her to have more."

Though Tony's words slurred around the edges, his logic made sense to Ben. His grandpa wanted to leave his fortune to the woman who amused him and provided him with companionship. Also, to the next generation of Crawfords, represented by his daughter.

Glancing at his wristwatch, Ben calculated the length of time his grandpa had been in surgery. Just over an hour. Too soon to expect results. "Let's hope Jerod will be around for many more years, and we won't have to worry about the will."

Without looking at him, Tony slid a one-page document across the bar toward him. "The Last Will and Testament of Charlene Elizabeth Belloc Crawford. She doesn't acknowledge any living relations. Leaves all her possessions to a couple of charities."

Ben read the pages. "The Retired Strippers League of Las Vegas?"

"Those were her roots." As he stared down into his glass, the creases near his eyes deepened as though he was holding back tears. "Charlene never pretended to be more than she was. Brassy, demanding and tough. But underneath it all... Underneath, she was a peach."

"You cared about her."

He drained the last of his vodka. "No more or less than any other client."

This half-drunk attempt at professionalism was unconvincing. Liz had caught him and Charlene groping each other in the hallway, and Ben was willing to bet that it hadn't been their first time. Tony might even have been falling in love with Jerod's wife. And that was a motive for murder.

Ben knew from his failed marriage that love could turn to hate in a twist of passion. If Tony had been rebuffed by Charlene, he might have wanted her dead.

Ben said, "Apparently, Charlene had a little something going with Ramon."

"Him? Not a chance."

"Ramon is a handsome guy." Ben hoped his comment

would provoke a reaction. "And passionate. Hell, he came after you with a knife."

"You don't need to remind me."

"Charlene liked him. Liked him a lot."

"He amused her." Tony shook his head, fighting off an alcoholic haze. "Told her some phony sob story. She gave him money." His fist came down hard on the bar. "I told her not to, but she laughed and said it wasn't a big deal. No biggie."

Ben waited for the lawyer to continue.

"That bastard," Tony muttered. "He used Charlene. Even got her to give him some of her jewelry. You know what I think?"

"No, Tony, I don't."

"I think that bastard stole some of Charlene's stuff. We ought to get the CBI to investigate Ramon."

"Why do you think Ramon stole Charlene's jewelry?"

"I was up in her room earlier. Doing an inventory, you know. For her will. I think some pieces are gone."

The potential theft of valuable jewelry shifted suspicion toward Ramon. Ben wished that Liz were here. He could have used her legal expertise in reading the will and her perceptions in reading Tony. When she was around, everything seemed more focused.

But the woman who sidled into the room was his sister. Apparently, Patrice had been eavesdropping because she jumped into the middle of the conversation. "You're right about Ramon. He's a despicable person. And there might have been another reason Charlene was giving him money."

"What's that?" Ben asked.

"Blackmail," she said darkly.

Before Ben could respond to his sister, he heard another

person coming down the stairs. Dr. Mancini offered a genial grin to the group. "It's a bit early to be gathering at the bar, folks."

Ben nodded a greeting. "Doctor."

"How's Jerod doing?"

"Too soon to know. He's still in surgery."

"As long as I'm here," Mancini said as he circled around the bar, "I might have one for the road. That's what we used to say back in the old days before DUIs. One for the road. Didn't seem like too much."

"Not anymore." Tony waggled a finger at him. "Drunk driving lands you in jail."

"Right you are, my friend." Mancini pulled a can of soda from the fridge. "I'll stick to a soft drink. You're all witnesses."

His sociable attitude should have been a refreshing change from the drunken angst of Tony Lansing and his sister's dire pronouncements. But Ben wasn't fooled by Mancini's bow ties and smiles. He'd seen the good doctor's aggressive side when he took fierce delight in destroying his tennis opponents; Mancini was in excellent physical condition for a man in his late fifties.

As Mancini popped the tab on his soda, he glanced toward Ben. "I stopped in to see your daughter a few days ago."

A jolt of alarm went through him. "Is Natalie ill?"

"Just a little summer cold. Nothing to worry about."

For some reason, he didn't like the idea of Mancini treating his daughter. When this was over, the doctor would be cut from all family business. "And you're here to see Patrice?"

"For my headache," she said. "I needed something stronger than aspirin."

"Always happy to oblige," Mancini said as he held up his old-fashioned doctor's bag.

Mancini was a walking pharmacy. Even if the CBI search turned up nothing unusual in the drugs they'd confiscated from the house, the doctor was here every day. And he didn't pay close attention to where he left his little black bag. Anybody and everybody in the household had ready access to those drugs.

Patrice tugged on his sleeve. "Ben, I need for you to listen to me. For once in your life, pay attention."

His supply of sympathy was running low, especially when it came to his sister. "What is it, Patrice?"

"Blackmail." She repeated the word quietly and pulled him a few steps away from the lawyer and doctor. "Like Charlene, I was making payments to Ramon. Nothing huge. Just enough to be irritating."

"For what?"

"An indiscretion." With a wave of her hand, she brushed away his question. "The important thing is that I don't want the CBI questioning Ramon. It would be dreadful to have my secrets known."

Especially while she was embarking on a career as a talk show guest. Her ability to stay completely focused on herself amazed and disgusted him. "How many other people was Ramon blackmailing?"

"Several," she said. "He certainly can't afford his lifestyle on the money he makes as a male model."

He couldn't imagine what Ramon might have on Charlene. The blond bombshell had always been open about her past "indiscretions." She was proud of her past; she'd named a retired stripper's fund in her will.

Glancing over his shoulder at the bar, he saw Mancini push a can of soda toward Tony. If the heartbroken lawyer had been having an affair with Charlene, she'd pay to keep that information from Jerod.

"All right, Patrice. What does your blackmail have to do with me?"

"I heard you and Tony talking. Ramon is about to become central in the murder investigation. You need to see Ramon before the CBI gets there. You have to, Ben. You have to get those photographs from Ramon."

His eyebrows raised. What had she done? "Photos?"

"I was young and stupid," she said. "I posed nude for a photographer."

"So what?" Naked pictures seemed appropriate for her new career as a tabloid darling.

"It was a long time ago, and I was…" She paused, scowling. "I was, well, plump."

Fat, nude photos of Patrice were so far down on his list of priorities that he almost laughed out loud. Being naked didn't bother her. But being pudgy?

He looked toward the door as Liz bounced into the room with her cell phone in hand. She beamed a grin as she came toward him. "Good news," she said.

"I could use some."

"Harry called with an update on Jerod. The operation is going better than expected. Zero complications from anesthetic. All systems are go."

"And the prognosis?"

She glanced between him and Patrice. "I keep trying to get these doctors to give me odds. Like Jerod is a ninety-to-one favorite for a full recovery. But they have their own language."

Dr. Mancini came out from behind the bar to join them. "What did they say?"

"Two words—cautious optimism." She addressed Mancini. "What does that mean?"

"The operation is going well, but they aren't making any promises." He patted Ben's shoulder. "You made the right decision."

It was a course of action Mancini could have supported a month ago, but Ben wasn't about to cast stones. His grandpa's recovery was all that mattered. He asked Liz, "When can we see him?"

"Two or three more hours. After the surgery, Jerod will be unconscious in Recovery."

"Oh, good," Patrice said as she grasped his arm. "That's enough time for you to take care of that other little problem we were talking about. Please, Ben."

His first priority was to be at the hospital. Everything else could wait. He linked his arm with Liz's and headed for the staircase. They were out of there.

Chapter Seventeen

"She tried to kill you with a flower box?"

"Not necessarily kill me," Liz said. "I think Annette just wanted me out of the way for a while so she could have a straight shot at you. Her Prince Charming."

Ben muttered, "I should have fired that loon first thing this morning."

She walked beside him on the city sidewalk outside Ramon's apartment building, glad that she'd changed out of her power suit and high heels into comfortable sneakers and jeans. "Maybe she deserved firing," she grudgingly admitted.

"Maybe? From what you just told me, Annette lied about seeing me carrying Charlene's body, took a valuable piece of jewelry as a bribe and tried to murder you." He smirked. "With a box of petunias."

Obviously, Annette wasn't a professional assassin. "She's valuable as a witness. And we need all the witnesses we can get. That's why we're here to see Ramon, right?"

"That's one reason. Another reason is Patrice. Another is that I can't stand waiting."

After spending an hour at the hospital, they'd determined there was nothing to be done but pacing and worrying. They'd decided to take action by coming to Ramon's upscale apartment building. The concierge told her that she'd seen Ramon in his running clothes and had assumed he was jogging in nearby Washington Park.

As they crossed the street into the park, she asked, "Why does Patrice want you to talk to Ramon?"

"You saw his apartment building."

"Nice place. Posh."

"And he drives a BMW. Dresses well."

She nodded. "Either Ramon has a trust fund or he's living way above the standard for a male model in Denver."

"According to my sister," Ben said, "his side employment is blackmail."

Given time and a bit of research on the Internet, Liz could have figured this out for herself. As would the CBI. Agent Lattimer would be all over Ramon Stephens after he talked to Annette.

They stood at the edge of the running path in the lush green park, landscaped leafy trees, shrubs and colorful gardens. The two lakes in the center of this acreage attracted flocks of ducks and hordes of waddling Canadian geese that honked aggressively at the many joggers, dog-walkers and young mothers pushing baby carriages.

The soles of Liz's feet itched to join in. She felt the need for speed. Ever since she'd found out that her suspicions of Ben were groundless, she'd been bubbling over with positive energy, and her physical attraction to him had become a palpable force.

Every time she looked at him, her mind went straight to the bedroom. Memories of their kisses in the forest played and replayed. The moonlight on his cheekbones.

The feel of his warm skin. His hard, muscular torso as he'd pressed against her.

She pushed those thoughts to the back of her mind. "Is Ramon blackmailing Patrice? What does he have on her?"

Ben lowered his sunglasses to look at her. "I shouldn't laugh. This is serious stuff to Patrice."

"What?" Liz had to know.

"Nudie photos." He couldn't help snickering. "My uptight sister had a moment of butt-naked wildness. And she wants those pictures back."

Ben's bodyguard stepped up beside them. "I suggest we go back to the vehicle, sir. This isn't a secure location."

"With all these people milling around?"

"Not to mention the geese," Liz said. "I've heard they can be good protectors."

The bodyguard did *not* crack a smile. "Look around. There's a lot of places where a sniper with a long-range rifle could take cover."

"I'll risk it," Ben said.

"It's my job to protect you, sir. I have to insist that we go back to the car."

On the far side of the lake near the boathouse, Liz spotted Ramon. At least, she thought it was him. Sleeveless white T-shirt. Baggy shorts. He ran at a careful pace as if each step was a pose for a commercial.

"You stay here," she said to Ben. "I'll talk to Ramon."

Before he could object, she took off running. Behind her, she heard the discussion between Ben and his bodyguard heating up. Not her problem. Nobody was trying to kill her. Not unless she counted crazy Annette.

Without thinking, Liz fell into her natural stride. Running was her second-favorite exercise. The martial arts, of course, came first. She circled the east side of the lake on the asphalt path, dodging around a very small woman struggling with the leash on a very big dog that apparently wanted to jump into the water.

As Liz approached the guy in the sleeveless T-shirt, she identified Ramon. His exertion showed in the sweat glistening on his chest and upper arms. With a sculpted body like his, she understood why some women found him attractive. He wasn't her type. Too pretty.

When he saw her, he made a quick pivot and went in the opposite direction.

Fine with her. Liz turned up the speed. Her sneakers pounded the asphalt path. "Hey, Ramon. Wait up."

He tossed a look over his shoulder and realized that she was closing the gap between them. To avoid being outrun by a girl, he slowed to a walk as she raced up beside him.

Glaring, he asked, "What do you want?"

"You're in big trouble." She kept pace beside him as they approached the boathouse and the playground on the opposite side. "Annette told me what happened on the night of the murder."

"Annette." He scoffed. "That's one messed-up chick."

"She's prepared to tell the CBI everything."

He stopped at the edge of the path. "That night, she was upset. I gave her a pin to make her feel better. Nothing wrong with that."

"A diamond pin," Liz said, "that belonged to Charlene."

"She gave it to me. As a gift."

"You take a lot of alleged gifts from women, Ramon."

And she was sure the CBI would drag all that information out of him when they investigated. She had a different agenda. "You know who murdered Charlene."

He inhaled, and his chest thrust out. Fists on hips, he

looked down at her with calculating eyes. In stark contrast to his fiery passion when he'd gone after Tony Lansing with a kitchen knife, his manner seemed cold and shrewd, like a con man about to close the deal. "Information like that could be worth something."

She couldn't believe he was suggesting blackmail. "I have no money. I was working as a maid. Remember?"

"Then I got no reason to talk to you."

"One question," she said. "That night at the party, why did you drug my drink?"

"You figure it out. You're the big detective."

How did he know she was a private investigator? That information could have only come from one source. "Victoria."

"Here's some questions for you," he said. "Free of charge."

"I'm listening."

"Who wanted Charlene dead so little Natalie could inherit big? Who wants sole custody of the kid? Who's willing to take a shot at Ben so he won't grab his share of the inheritance?"

She repeated the name. "Victoria."

Ramon sneered. "But we both know that she's not a killer."

She glanced over her shoulder and saw Ben and his bodyguard approaching. "Ramon, tell me who?"

She didn't hear the snap of the rifle. There were no warning reports.

Ramon staggered back. His arms flapped helplessly at his sides. Blood stained the front of his white T-shirt.

His knees buckled, and he sank to the ground.

She whirled and stared, trying to spot the gleam of sunlight on a long-distance rifle. Where was the sniper?

In the trees? In one of the nearby apartment buildings? Leaning out of a car window?

She heard Ben call her name, and her self-preservation instincts kicked in. She dropped to the ground in a low crouch next to Ramon. Blood was everywhere. Soaking his shirt. Staining his hands. Dribbling from the corner of his mouth. As she watched, his chest went still. His eyes stared sightlessly at the blue Colorado sky.

Her mind blanked. All rational thought recoiled. Though she was in the middle of this horrible scene, she felt distant and unconnected.

Ben was beside her. His arms encircled her, pulling her away from the body and protecting her at the same time. Behind him, the bodyguard had drawn his weapon and shouted at others to get down.

The pleasant spring day at the park turned into a nightmare. Joggers reacted with screams. Mothers gathered their babies from carriages and ran. The big white dog broke free from his owner and plunged into the lake. A flock of geese took off in a *V* and arrowed across the sky.

"Liz." Ben shook her. "Liz, are you all right?"

Unable to speak, she nodded dumbly.

"Can you walk?"

Without waiting for her reply, he lifted her from the ground and carried her around the edge of the lake to the boathouse. As they stepped into the shaded pavilion, hidden from the sniper by wide stucco arches, she regained her senses.

Her arms coiled around his neck. "You can put me down now."

When her feet touched the concrete floor, her legs were steady enough to support her weight. Still, she clung to him.

The bodyguard checked them both. Gun still in hand, he instructed, "Stay here. The police are on the way."

Ben leaned back against the stucco wall, and she leaned against him, weakened and stunned. She'd been the same way when they'd found Charlene's body. There was something horrible and shocking about violent death.

"I should be tougher." She had a black belt in karate, could handle herself in dangerous situations. "I think it's the blood. I hate blood."

With a gentle caress, he cupped her chin and turned her face toward his. His gaze examined her, looking for signs of damage. "I shouldn't have brought you here. I wasn't aware of the risk."

"Not your fault." She hadn't recovered enough to smile. "This sniper. Was he the same guy?"

"I didn't hear a gunshot. The sniper must have used a long-distance rifle with a silencer. The same type of weapon as the guy who shot at us."

But he hadn't been aiming at Ben. Or at her. "Ramon was the target."

"This time, he might have blackmailed the wrong person."

From a distance, she heard the scream of police sirens as they converged on the park. She buried her face in the soft cotton of Ben's blue workshirt and closed her eyes, wishing they could be alone, wishing with all her heart that Ramon's murder had never happened.

Chapter Eighteen

In the relative quiet of the hospital waiting area, Ben sat beside Liz. Waiting. The doctors said Jerod's operation had gone well; they had eradicated the tumor in his brain. But it was taking him a long time to come out of the anesthetic. Possible outcomes ranged from full recovery for Jerod to having him in a coma state.

And there was nothing Ben could do about it. The helplessness was killing him, tying his gut in a knot. When Liz touched his arm, he startled. "What?"

"Do you want coffee?"

"Do you?"

"No." She offered a tense smile. "It seems like the thing to do when you're nervous. A cup of coffee. Or tea. Or a triple shot of Jack Daniel's."

"Spoken like a bartender."

She reached behind her shoulder and patted herself on the back. "Just one of my many skills."

He was glad to see her making jokes again. Her near collapse at the boathouse had scared him. But Liz was resilient.

If he focused on her, he might stay sane in the midst of this endless waiting. He stared at her for a moment, counting the many shades of blond and brown in her choppy hair, noticing the light spray of freckles across her nose. Tonight, he hoped she would sleep in his bed. If she only wanted to cuddle, he'd restrain himself. If she wanted more, he would gladly comply.

"I know what you need," she said. "Close your eyes and think of sailing."

"I'd rather look at you."

"You need to relax. You're so tense."

"Who wouldn't be? Grandpa's hovering between life and death, and I just witnessed a murder. Not to mention being the primary suspect in a CBI investigation."

His whole life was in chaos, and Ben prided himself on staying in control. When ill winds blew, he held fast to the rudder and steered through the storm. In those moments of peril when the waves splashed high and swamped the decks, he held firm.

He didn't blame himself for Ramon's murder. The blackmailing male model had tried to run a scam on a killer and had paid the ultimate price. There was nothing Ben could have done to change the outcome.

Nor was he responsible for Charlene's death.

Unfortunately, he wasn't sure others would agree. Especially not Lattimer.

Ben looked down the sterile hospital corridor and saw the CBI agent stalking toward them. Lattimer's demeanor was nowhere near as well groomed as usual. The knot on his necktie yanked to the left. The carry strap for his laptop computer slipped off his shoulder. His jaw clenched so tightly that he could have been grinding rocks with his back molars.

"He looks mad," Liz whispered. "I can't believe I'm saying this, but do you want me to call your lawyer?"

"I'll handle this." Ben stood to face the CBI agent.

Lattimer spoke first. "Mr. Crawford, I have given you every consideration. Kept you updated. Allowed you to stay in the comfort of your own home rather than taking you to an interrogation room. And what happens? How do you pay me back? You get involved in another murder."

"Didn't plan it that way," Ben said.

"When the CBI is called in on a case, we maintain control of the jurisdiction. I had to spend the last two hours with the DPD, SWAT and NSA-trained officers who thought they were facing a terrorist attack."

That seemed far-fetched. "From snipers in Washington Park?"

"Four people were injured while they fled. Nothing serious. Nothing that required hospitalization." The vein in Lattimer's forehead began to throb. "One woman almost drowned while trying to rescue her dog."

Though Ben regretted the disturbance, he wasn't about to apologize. *This wasn't his fault.* "The next time I run into a sneak ambush from a sniper, I'll let you know ahead of time."

"There had better not be a next time," Lattimer said. "I strongly suggest that you return to the house where you and your family are under the protection of a top-notch security team. Got it? Stay out of my investigation."

Ben wasn't in the mood to take orders. He'd cooperated with the police every step of the way, hadn't ordered his lawyers to block the search warrant. He'd kept quiet…until now. "Your investigation, Agent Lattimer, doesn't exactly qualify as a big success."

"Excuse me?"

"As a businessman, I measure achievement in results. Tangible profit and advances. Far as I can see, you've got nothing." He ignored Lattimer's sputtering objections. "You wasted time and resources by suspecting me, trying to put together a case against me. You skipped over other possibilities."

"Don't tell me how to do my job."

"Did you know Ramon Stephens was a blackmailing son-of-a-bitch? Did you look into his finances?" That should have been an obvious lead. "When Annette started babbling about monsters in the night, you bought it. Instead of poking holes in her story, you believed I was the monster."

"Annette," he said disgustedly.

"You've talked to her. Right?"

His answer was to set his laptop computer down on one of the chairs and flip it open. Liz left her seat and came forward to better view the screen.

"I went to the house to interview Annette," Lattimer said. "She was already gone."

"No way," Liz said. "I left her with the security guard."

"She went up to her room, supposedly to change clothes, slipped out the window and was in her car at the gate before anybody could notify them that she wasn't allowed to leave."

He pressed the play button on the computer. "This video came from the surveillance tape at the gate."

Ben watched the screen and saw Annette lean through the open window of her car and look directly into the camera.

"Should have fired that loon," Ben muttered.

"We'll find her," Lattimer said. "And we'll verify what Liz told me about her change in story."

"About Ramon and the diamond brooch," Liz said. "I

told the policeman who took my statement what Ramon said. About Victoria."

"I have a copy of your statement."

"I can't believe she's a killer," Liz said.

Ben wasn't so sure. He'd seen his estranged wife fly into a murderous rage. It unsettled him to think that Victoria was behind these murders. Thank God, Natalie was coming to stay with him tomorrow.

"I'm stepping up the investigation on Victoria," Lattimer said. "Checking her finances and connections. I'll handle this. In the meantime, I want you both to return to the house and stay put."

"That doesn't work for me," Ben said. "I'll need to be coming in and out of town to see my grandfather."

"How's he doing?"

"We're still waiting to find out."

Lattimer's hostility decreased a few notches. "This is rough on you. I hope your grandfather is all right."

"Thanks."

When he held out his hand, Lattimer shook it. They had come to an understanding.

"One more thing," Liz piped up. "Is Ben still your favorite suspect? Or not so much?"

"The latter." Lattimer packed up his laptop. "Stay safe."

Ben barely had a chance to sit when Harry Schooner came into the waiting room and motioned for them to follow him. "Looks like Jerod's about to wake up."

Ben jumped to his feet. The tension that had been building since his grandpa went into the hospital tightened around his spine. Stiffly, he walked beside Liz. Hoping for the best. Fearing the worst.

Harry shuffled along behind them. "The docs say you can see him for five minutes. Then not until tomorrow."

"Right."

They paused at the window of the ICU recovery room where Jerod was hooked up to IVs and monitors that recorded his blood pressure and heartbeat. His surgeon stood beside him, motioning them to step forward.

"Five minutes," he said.

The moment Ben touched his grandpa's hand, he felt a twitch in response. A good sign. Jerod looked like hell. Every wrinkle deepened to a crevasse. His skin was pale as a sheet of paper. He licked his lips.

"Grandpa," Ben whispered, "do you want some water?"

"Cold beer."

Those two words lifted the darkness. Jerod was going to survive. He'd be okay.

Slowly, his eyelids raised. He focused. Really focused on Ben's face. "You need a haircut, boy."

"You can see me?"

"Hell, yes."

Jerod's gaze shifted. He stared at Harry. Then at Liz. Finally, he looked at Ben again. "Where's Charlene?"

Ben's heart clenched.

"That's long enough," the doctor said. "Jerod needs his rest. We still have a number of tests to run."

Ben leaned down and kissed Jerod's forehead. "I love you."

He'd do anything to spare his grandpa the terrible sorrow of losing his wife. But there was no way to avoid the truth.

NIGHT SETTLED HEAVILY AT THE Crawford estate. As the long shadows of the forest closed in on the tiered cedar house, Liz sat cross-legged in the center of the narrow bed in her garret. Her stomach growled. All she'd had for dinner was a couple of granola bars because she preferred not to sit across the dining room table from Patrice and Monte. Nor did she want to chat with the staff, especially not Rachel: It wouldn't be much fun to tell the housekeeper that her dear friend, Victoria, was likely involved in a murder plot.

As for Ben? He was brooding. In a dark funk, he'd sequestered himself in his workshop with his boat. She understood his pain. Telling Jerod the truth about Charlene would be terrible.

She checked her wristwatch. Nine o'clock. Ben had locked himself away for two-and-a-half hours. She should go to the log barn and see him. As his personal assistant, it was her duty to keep him on track and focused.

But the honest-to-goodness reason she wanted to see Ben had nothing to do with solving a crime or tending to business. After last night's interrupted passion, she wanted a second chance.

She kneaded her fingers in the bedspread, holding on tightly. Making love to him wasn't rational. When this investigation was over, she would return to her world, which was far, far away from the lifestyles of the rich and semi-famous. She and Ben weren't relationship material.

And there was also the matter of her deception. The big, fat lie. When he found out that she came here under false pretenses and was really working for Victoria, he wouldn't want anything to do with her.

But for tonight? She didn't have to tell him. For tonight, they could offer each other the comfort and solace they both needed. They could finally act on the intense magnetism that drew them together.

She should take this night. One night with him.

Before she could change her mind, she hopped off the bed, grabbed her denim jacket and flung open the door. Charging down the staircase, she remembered her first day as a maid and Rachel's comment that she made too much noise. Very true. Liz was loud and abrupt and not very cultured. But Ben wanted her all the same. She knew he did.

At the front door, she encountered one of the security men, clad in a dark gray G.I. Joe outfit with combat boots. "Where are you headed?" he asked.

"Is Ben still in the log barn?"

"The murder scene?" He nodded. "Yeah, he's there."

"That's where I'm going."

"I'll take you." G.I. Joe accompanied her down the hill toward the barn. Though he had a flashlight, it wasn't needed. The waning moon provided enough light to see all the way to the front gate, which was blessedly vacant. At this hour, the reporters had retired.

The closer they got to the log barn,, the more she wondered if she was making a mistake. Ben had a right to his privacy. But what about her rights? What about the unspoken promise of last night?

If he didn't want to see her, he'd tell her to leave, and that would be that.

Another security guard was posted outside the log barn. When she approached, he gave her a nod, twisted the knob and opened the door.

Too late to turn back.

She stepped inside. Her gaze went to the spot where they'd found Charlene's body. Instead of a chalk outline of the victim, the concrete floor had been scrubbed clean. Not a single trace of blood remained.

Ben gave her a glance, then returned to his work. With long smooth strokes, he sanded the white oak. "Is there a problem?"

"Not really."

"You could have called me on the cell phone."

But she had wanted to see him. Even if the rest of the night didn't go the way she'd planned, it was worth it. His gray T-shirt outlined his arms and shoulders as he stroked the curved line of the hull. His jeans hung low on his hips. There was nothing like watching a man doing physical labor to remind a woman why the opposite sex was so very useful.

She stepped up beside him and glided her fingers across the satin-smooth wood. "It's beautiful."

"She's coming along." He stepped back to admire his handiwork. "I had hoped to have her finished before Natalie's visit. That's not going to happen."

"You'll have plenty of time. The whole rest of the summer. You and Jerod can both teach her how to sail."

"He's going to be all right."

But she heard the doubt in his voice. He wasn't referring to Jerod's recovery from the operation. The emotional pain of losing Charlene would be hard to bear.

Her gaze fell to the floor where they'd found the body. Cleaning up the bloodstains didn't erase the memory.

Ben touched her cheek and turned her face toward him. "Why did you come down here?"

Her heart skipped a couple of beats. Usually, she was fairly direct with men. Came right out and told them what she wanted. But this was different.

Digging into the pocket of her denim jacket, she pulled out her last granola bar. "I brought you dinner."

A slow grin teased the corners of his mouth, and his eyes took on a sexy glow. "I don't believe you."

"True story."

"I wanted you to come to me. I wished it."

"How much?"

"A lot," he said.

"Show me."

His embrace sent her pulse racing. The pressure of his lips against hers sparked a sensual heat that burned slowly through her veins. In about two seconds, she was ready to tear off her clothes.

Gasping, she asked, "Condom?"

"No."

She wasn't about to go through the same thing that happened last night. "Race you back to the house."

Chapter Nineteen

Holding Liz's hand, Ben ran up the hill toward the house. His armed bodyguard followed, hand on weapon and not amused. By contrast, he and Liz were giggling like a couple of teenagers on a first date. Inside the front door, he aimed for the front stairs, and she followed.

Upstairs in his bedroom, they grabbed for each other. Her arms wrapped around his neck, pulling him close for another deep, fierce kiss. He held her tight with one arm. His other hand cupped her round bottom, anchoring her.

The pressure inside him began to build as her body rocked against him. What they lacked in subtlety, they made up for in passion.

He needed this release, this moment of mind-numbing, heart-pumping lust. But he had to slow down. If he continued at this pace, he'd be done before he got her clothes off. And he wanted more for her. A night for the record books.

Grasping her shoulders, he forced her away from him. Her cheeks flushed a delicious pink. Her lips parted, and she was breathing hard.

He peeled off her denim jacket and threw it aside. In a belated attempt to be suave, he unfastened the first button on her blouse and lightly caressed her creamy skin.

"Too slow," she said.

"Give me time, Liz."

She tore open the buttons on her shirt. The fabric slipped from her shoulders. Her torso was smooth and firm with a feminine curve at her waist. Beautiful as a marble sculpture. Why did she hide this body under baggy shirts? He reached behind her back and unhooked her lacy white bra. Dusky rose nipples tipped her firm, round breasts.

When he leaned down and suckled, she arched her back, trembled and moaned. The sound aroused him. He wanted to feed her hunger, to satisfy her completely. She was more to him than a wild one-night stand. A hell of a lot more.

Liz stood by him when no one else would. She was steadfast and strong. His woman.

He tore off his shirt, and they joined in an embrace. Flesh to flesh, the friction of their bodies sparked a tactile sensation of driving heat that grew more and more intense. Explosive. Combustible.

They fell back onto the bed, shedding the rest of their clothing in a frenzy. He threw back the covers, and she stretched out on the sheets. Her shapely legs moved languidly. With a pointed toe, she traced a line down the center of his chest. He grasped her foot, kissed the sole, then the knee. His fingers parted the delicate folds at the juncture of her thighs. She was hot and wet, ready for him. Waiting for him. But not patiently.

She sat up on the bed, wrapped her arms around him and fell back, pulling him down on top of her in a neat and effective maneuver. She was a demanding lover. He liked that.

Her fingers slid down his body, lower and lower until she grasped his hardness. Slowly, enticingly, she tugged.

Electricity crackled beneath the surface of his skin. He was about to explode, needed for her to stop, wanted her to keep going.

Frantically, he tugged open the drawer of his bedside table. He found his supply of condoms. As he sheathed himself, she caressed his arms, his chest, his shoulders.

"Faster," she urged him.

"I was thinking I might get the whipped cream."

"Later."

Her urgency spurred him to action. He rose above her, positioned himself between her widespread thighs.

For a moment, he paused as he gazed down into her wide green eyes. He caressed her gently, savoring the anticipation of the moment when they would join.

"Now," she said. "Now, Ben."

As if there were any doubt.

He plunged into her, and she closed tightly around him. So tight. So perfect.

She matched the rhythm of his thrusts, taking all of him into her body. Never before had he been with a woman whose hunger matched his own. It took all of his self-control to hold back. Her gasps turned into little yips. He waited. It was impossible. He waited until he felt her convulsing. Then he allowed himself to take his sweet, shuddering release.

He collapsed on the bed beside her. In spite of every other disaster that plagued his life, he was happy. Fulfilled. At peace.

Quiet now, they held each other. As a general rule, he wasn't big on talking after sex, but he needed to let her know how important she was to him. He cared about her, wanted to spend a hell of a lot more time with her. Days and weeks. Maybe even years.

Though he might love her, he didn't dare say the word out loud. It was too soon.

After a contented sigh, she propped herself up on an elbow and looked down at him. Her contented smile was more enigmatic than the Mona Lisa's. "Ben," she said.

"Yes, Liz."

She reached across the covers and picked up his black boxers, which she dangled from the waistband. "Why am I not surprised that these are silk?"

"So are your panties."

"Very true." Liz liked to indulge herself with quality undergarments. "Under our clothes, I guess we're both millionaires."

She dropped the boxers, hoping that he wouldn't bother putting them on. He had one of the all-time best bodies she'd ever seen. A broad, firm chest with exactly the right amount of hair. A long, lean middle. And a tight butt.

She couldn't stop looking at him. He pleased her in every way. Even better, he was a skilled lover who knew when to thrust hard and when to tease.

If this night had been *only* about sex, she would have been coolly, blissfully happy. But there was something more. In the midst of their crazy wild passion, for one special moment, he'd looked into her eyes, and they'd connected at a deep level. More than lovers? That scared her.

He glided his finger through her hair. "There's something I want to ask you."

This could be trouble. "Ben, we really don't have to talk. I'm not—"

"How would you like a promotion?"

"What?"

"You heard me." He kissed her forehead. "I value your intelligence and efficiency. I want you with me on a more permanent basis."

"With full benefits?"

"The fullest." His sexy grin sent a shiver down her backbone.

She didn't know what to make of his offer. "After sex, most guys want to go steady or something like that. But you're offering a job? It almost feels like you're paying me to make love."

"I can't put a price on what happened between us tonight."

"Even with your millions, you couldn't afford me." She rubbed up against his chest. "The only way you get that kind of passion is free."

But there was no way she could accept his offer. She'd intended to return any paycheck he might have cut for her. It was unethical to accept because Liz was already on the job, and Victoria was paying the tab. After she revealed that bit of info, she doubted he'd ever want her around on a permanent basis. "You told Lattimer that you based success on tangible results."

"True."

"We still haven't figured out who murdered Charlene. I mean, we've pushed your name off the top of the CBI's list of suspects, but we still don't know."

"And I need that answer," he said. "Jerod will want to see Charlene's killer brought to justice."

"Here's my proposal," she said. "When I've figured out the crime, I'll have a proven success record. And I'll be worthy of a promotion."

"Fair enough."

He leaned forward to seal their bargain with a kiss, and

she gladly joined her lips with his. His scent intoxicated her senses, and she knew they would be making love again tonight.

But not right now. Though she didn't have the yellow legal pad with her notes, she ran through the list of suspects in her head. Patrice and Monte. Tony Lansing. Dr. Mancini. Victoria. And an array of others who hated Charlene, including party guests and staff at the house.

"Right now, I'm most curious about Victoria," she said.

"Lattimer is investigating her."

"He should be. Ramon clearly implicated her, and I could easily see someone like Victoria hiring a sniper. Still, I don't think she killed Charlene."

"God, I hope not. Not matter what I think of my soon-to-be-ex-wife, she's still the mother of my child."

"She could have talked Tony into the murder. As the family attorney, he'd have a lot of influence in handling Jerod's estate when it passes to Natalie."

"Which," Ben said, "won't be for several years. Jerod is going to recover."

Ironically, Jerod's probable recovery from the tumor changed the motivation for Charlene's murder. The killer had acted within hours of the new will being filed to make sure that Charlene would predecease Jerod. If she hadn't stood in the way of his operation, she might still be alive today.

She finished off a peach and washed it down with a sip of bottled water. "I'll make nice with Agent Lattimer tomorrow. He might have more information."

"That reminds me," Ben said. "He called on my cell while I was working on the boat. The CBI warranted search of the house didn't turn up the sedative used on Charlene."

Which was probably the same drug Ramon had slipped into her drink. She sensed that Ben wasn't telling her everything. "What else?"

"They did find tablets that matched the autopsy report."

"At Ramon's," she assumed.

He nodded. "That particular sedative was also in the black bag Dr. Mancini carries on his house calls."

THE NEXT MORNING, LIZ DIDN'T want to leave his bed. She hated the chirping birds and the morning light that slid over the windowsill. This might be the last time, the only time, she would wake up and find Ben beside her.

She had to tell him about being a P.I., couldn't allow the lie to continue for one more day. Then, he'd hate the sight of her. She'd have to leave him, would never feel his kisses again, would never spend another night making love.

She watched his profile as he slept. Even in repose, he had an intensity that compelled her toward him. She'd tried to shield her heart by telling herself that a relationship between them would never work. They came from different worlds. She'd tried to fight the magnetism, but she'd been swept away. Oh, God, she would miss this man.

His eyelids opened, and a lazy morning grin spread across his face. With a growl, he pulled her close and kissed her forehead. "Glad you're here. Thought maybe I dreamed you."

"I'm real."

He rolled over to look at the bedside clock. "Damn. It's after eight. I need to be at the hospital."

Today, he would tell his grandpa about Charlene's murder. "Do you want me to come with you?"

"This is something I should do alone."

She understood. This was a pain that couldn't be shared. "I wish you didn't have to tell him."

"Me, too."

"If his vision hadn't cleared up, I would have pretended to be Charlene forever. Even if I can't stand that perfume."

"There's no way around it." He stared up at the ceiling. "It's always best to tell the truth."

Not always. When she told him the truth, their budding relationship would explode in a giant fireball. She'd never asked to care about him, never wanted to know how perfectly they fit together. And now, her unrequited dreams would be incinerated.

She decided against telling him now. The emotional devastation of dealing with Jerod was enough for one morning. Instead, she got dressed and went downstairs to the dining room while Ben took his shower.

Breakfast at the Crawford estate was never a formal affair. People wandered in and out of the kitchen, choosing whatever they wanted. Three security guards sat at the table, digging into fluffy omelets and bacon.

In the kitchen, Rachel helped the chef by washing plates. Coldly, she asked, "Did you sleep well?"

"Very." Liz wasn't intimidated. "Looks like you could use a hand."

"Annette had her problems, but she was a good maid. Did as she was told."

"Not like me," Liz said.

"Not in the least."

She pitched in and helped with the household chores while Ben was driven to the hospital by one of the security men.

As she swept the deck outside Jerod's room, Liz turned her thoughts to the murder investigation. Though Ramon hadn't admitted that he'd drugged her and Charlene, she started with that assumption. And the drugs had come from Dr. Mancini's bag.

Mancini could have paid Ramon to make sure that she and Charlene were both knocked out. But why?

Mancini could have also returned to the house and turned off the security camera. Was he the killer?

Her cell phone buzzed. It was Harry, calling from the hospital.

"Wanted you to know," he said. "Jerod's okay. He's got a bad case of broken heart, but all his other systems are working just fine."

"Ben had to tell him about the murder."

"It took courage to talk to his grandpa, but it was the right thing to do."

"It's always best to tell the truth."

No matter how devastating.

Chapter Twenty

Ben strode through the front door with only one thought in mind. *Find Liz.* He needed her.

In the study, he walked directly into her embrace. In silence, they held each other. He drew warmth from her breath, solace from her touch, strength from her endless supply of spirit. He stood there for several long minutes, reviving himself.

When he loosened his hold, she led him to the sofa and held his hand while he sat.

"Talking to Jerod," he said quietly. "It ripped me apart."

His grandpa was still weak, and the medications made him dizzy. But his vision had returned, and he was clearly on the mend. Then Ben gave him the news. "The light in his eyes went out. I could see his sorrow."

"You had to do it."

"No other way," he agreed. "He's being moved to a private room later today. As soon as he starts watching the television, he'll see all about our high profile murder."

"Did you tell him about me impersonating Charlene?"

"Actually, that was the one bright moment. Jerod's fire came back. He was so damn angry. If he'd been strong enough, he would have climbed out of that hospital bed and kicked my ass."

"Doesn't sound too cheerful."

"I'd rather see him fighting mad than drowning in sorrow. Your pal, Harry, agrees. He's a hell of a nice guy. A good companion for Jerod."

"He likes you, too. He called and told me."

"You never mentioned that he runs a private detective agenda. Maybe we should hire him to investigate the murder."

"There's a thought."

His gaze sank into her jade eyes, and he saw that she was troubled. Who wouldn't be? Together, they had experienced a lifetime in the past few days. Tragedy, fear and pain. On the plus side was Jerod's recovery. And last night's lovemaking. Love? That word kept popping into his head. *Love.* When he was with Liz, no other description applied.

All his life, he'd been running the family businesses and protecting their interests. Sure, he knew how to delegate, but the only person he could count on was himself. And now, there was Liz. He trusted her implicitly.

"We've all got to pull together," he said as he stood. "Natalie will be here any minute."

"It occurred to me that I've never seen her room. I've been all over the house with cleaning and such, but never there."

"I'm sure she'll show it to you."

They went upstairs to the deck outside Jerod's room to watch for the car that would bring his daughter to him. She was only supposed to stay for three days, but he was hoping for a longer visit.

Liz leaned her back against the railing and looked up at him. "I've been trying to figure out the murder. Dr. Mancini looks real guilty to me, but he doesn't have a motive."

Apparently, she was taking her self-imposed task of investigating seriously. "You're focused on Mancini because the sedative used on Charlene was in his possession, but that doesn't mean he used them. He always leaves his bag lying around. Anybody could have gotten hold of those sedatives. Maybe Ramon was acting on his own."

"Not for free," she said. "I don't think Ramon ever did anything without a price. The killer—whoever it was— paid Ramon to drug the drinks and to plant that lie in Annette's mind."

Ben saw the front gates open. Natalie was here.

When the car pulled up, he yanked open the back door and helped his five-year-old daughter out of her car seat. She hugged him and giggled. There was no more beautiful sound in the world than the laughter of a child.

Every time he saw his beautiful daughter, he marveled. She had her mother's thick, black hair, but her blue eyes matched his own.

When he introduced her to Liz, Natalie politely shook hands and said, "*Buenos dias*. I know Spanish. Nanny is teaching me."

"*¿Como esta?*" Liz asked.

"*Muy bueno,*" Natalie said very seriously. "Do you know any other languages?"

"A little bit of Japanese," Liz said. "I teach at a karate school, and some of my students are your age."

"A boy in my class knows karate. He's a big show-off. Can you teach me how to beat him up?"

"Maybe later," Ben said as he stepped in. "Liz has never seen your room. Would you show her around?"

Natalie linked her hand with Liz's and started toward the house. His daughter was chatty and smart, but not annoying. She'd never turned into one of those kids who were like performing seals, demanding attention for all their tricks. Natalie knew how to watch and learn.

He wanted to teach her everything, especially how to sail. When she was a baby, he'd taken her for swimming lessons and she had done him proud. Had taken to the water like a baby otter.

His cares and worries faded in the glow of innocence from his child. She brightened the world around her. Even Patrice and Monte smiled in her presence. Rachel nearly smothered the child in a gigantic bear hug.

Natalie's happiness was the only thing that mattered. Everything else would sort itself out.

After Natalie had showed off her room, Ben escorted his daughter and Liz down to the workshop to check on the progress of the boat. The name of this craft had already been decided by his daughter; it would be christened *Fifi* after her favorite stuffed animal.

He liked the way Liz interacted with Natalie. Not at all condescending or forced. They seemed to honestly enjoy each other. He took pleasure in seeing them joke and talk and flip stones into the lake. For a few sunlit hours, it felt like they were a family. A real family.

Around three o'clock, Natalie had begun to wilt. He picked her up, gave her a kiss on the tip of her nose and said, "Nap time."

"Daddy." Natalie rolled her eyes. "I don't do naps."

"That's not what your mom told me. She said you had a cold and needed to rest."

"She just said that because Dr. Mancini told her to. It's a little cold." She squeezed her fingers together. "Very little."

"When did you see the doctor?"

"All the time." Another eye roll. "He mostly comes to see my mommy. But sometimes, me."

"Dr. Mancini seems nice," Liz said. "Do you like him?"

"Mommy does. She likes him a bunch."

The farthest thing from Ben's mind was probing his daughter for information to use in their investigation. But this revelation could not be ignored. If Victoria and Mancini were having an affair, the doctor had a motive for wanting Charlene dead.

Dr. Mancini with his innocent white hair and bow ties didn't seem like the type to be carried away by passion. But Victoria preferred men with money. Like doctors.

After he told Liz to wait for him in the study, Ben took Natalie upstairs to her bedroom at the top of the stairs, where she negotiated her way out of a nap. This would be an hour of quiet time.

Surrounded by half a dozen stuffed animals, she lay down on her bed, and he told her a story. By the end, she was fast asleep. Her thick black eyelashes formed sweet crescents on her rosy cheeks.

He needed to do a better job of protecting her. If Victoria and Mancini had been plotting murder and hiring snipers, Ben would never allow Natalie to return to his estranged wife's house. He needed to report this information to Agent Lattimer as soon as possible. Get the investigation moving in the right direction.

In the study, Liz stood waiting for him. The afternoon sunlight through the window struck highlights in her hair. Her gaze cast down. "Ben, there's something I need to tell you."

"It'll have to wait." He reached for the phone on the desktop. "I need put in a call to Lattimer."

She caught hold of his wrist. "Believe me, I'd love to wait. But I have to tell you now."

He gave her his full attention. Whatever she had to say was important to her. "I'm listening."

"When I came to this house, I expected you to be a spoiled, insensitive jerk who never did an honest day's work. I never wanted to care about you."

"But you do care."

"God help me, I do. That's why this is so hard."

He saw the pain in her eyes and stepped toward her, hoping to offer comfort. But she braced her arm straight in front of her, holding him back.

"Let me finish," she said. "Posing as a maid was an undercover assignment. I'm really a private investigator, working for Harry Schooner."

His rational mind couldn't accept what she was saying. "What were you here to investigate?"

"You."

The word plunged a knife in his gut. "Why?"

"Credible information that you were a drug user. I was here to get tangible proof that could be used in court." A ragged breath rattled through her. "To prove that you were an unfit father."

He remembered the custody battle. The knife twisted. "Victoria hired you."

"I thought I was doing the right thing, protecting a child from an addict father. On the night you made that drug buy in Denver, I was on the street watching. I saw you give money to that dealer. I saw you take the merchandise."

"Drugs for Jerod."

"I know." A tear spilled down her cheek. "Now, I know."

"You spied on me in Denver. Then you came here to betray me." Everything about her was a lie. "You wanted me to lose custody of my child."

"I couldn't make sense of what I'd seen. I knew you trafficked with drug dealers. But I also knew you were a decent man. That's why I left."

"And why did you come back?"

"I didn't want to. Victoria was offering a lot of money, and Harry really needs a big payoff. He wants to retire, and I couldn't—"

"Why?" he demanded.

"I wanted to solve the murder. Ben, I wasn't lying when I said that I believed in your innocence. I know you're not a killer."

"No more goddamned excuses, Liz." Nothing could make him forgive her. "Why are you back here?"

"Victoria wanted me to return."

"You're still working for her."

"Yes," she said.

The air went out of her, and she seemed to collapse within herself. But he had no sympathy for her and her crocodile tears. He had trusted her, and she paid him back with a heartless deception.

He wanted to hate her, but the rage that surged within him was as much for himself as for her. God, he was a fool.

"I should have guessed," he said. "The way you stepped in and separated Tony and Ramon was too…professional."

"I'm sorry."

"You were too slick when you pretended to be Charlene. Right away, you picked up on her voice and her mannerisms. Just another undercover job for you."

"I wanted to help."

"How about last night? When you went to bed with me, that must have been part of your plan. I hope Victoria pays you extra for that."

"Last night." She lifted her chin. "It was wrong of me to want you. But I did. More than my principles. More than anything. I don't regret one minute."

"Get the hell out of my sight."

Without another word, she walked through the door.

Chapter Twenty-One

Numbly, Liz climbed the stairs to her garret bedroom and gathered her things. She couldn't blame Ben for hating her. She had come here under false pretenses, intending to betray him. There was no pretty way to explain it.

She was in the wrong. And she'd lost everything. The future, which would have been bright with him, had turned into a gaping, dark abyss. She needed to get away from here. To put a million miles between herself and the man she could have loved.

In the third floor hallway with her gym bag in her hand, she paused outside the door to Rachel's room. She probably ought to inform her of what had happened. Though Liz hadn't mentioned Rachel's name, Ben might have questions for the housekeeper.

Liz tapped lightly. "Rachel?"

She pushed the door open to peek inside and caught a whiff of the heavy floral scent she'd come to hate. Charlene's cologne. God, that stuff was strong. She sniffed again. Was she imagining the stink? Liz was so attuned to the guilt she felt for wearing that cologne to play her role as Charlene, that it was branded in her olfactory memory.

She entered the room, which was three times as large as her own tiny garret. When she opened the closet, she spotted a pair of sneakers—huge, probably a size twelve. When Liz held them to her nose, they smelled like Charlene. Stuffed in the bottom of a laundry bag was a pair of black slacks and a sweater. On the shelf above the clothing rack, she found a black knit cap.

Everything became clear.

Rachel had gone into Dr. Mancini's bag and stolen the sedatives. She must have paid Ramon to slip the drug into Liz's drink because Rachel had known Liz was an investigator.

Then Ramon had drugged Charlene.

Rachel knew about Annette's night wandering. She'd arranged with Ramon to poison Annette's mind.

With easy access to all the household keys, Rachel had gone to the surveillance shed and turned off the camera. She had gone to Charlene's room. They'd struggled. The bottle of cologne had shattered, and the smell had been everywhere.

Big, tall Rachel had carried Charlene's body to the log barn. And she'd committed murder.

Liz looked up in time to see Rachel barreling across the room. She'd come out of nowhere. For such a big woman, she was incredibly light on her feet. She swung hard with a heavy object. A tool? Though Liz dodged, she took a glancing blow to the forehead, enough to knock her down. The inside of her head exploded with pain.

She had to get up, had to defend herself. Couldn't move.

Rachel plunged a hypodermic needle into her arm and retreated, giving her plenty of space. Triumphant, she said, "You'll be unconscious in two minutes."

Enough time to call for help. Enough time to make one assault. Liz staggered to her feet. The room whirled like an insane carousel. She was already light-headed. Struggling, she managed to speak. "Why did you kill Charlene?"

"Because Victoria is my friend. With that bitch Charlene out of the way, our little Natalie will inherit."

"You framed Ben."

"He doesn't deserve custody."

Clinging to the edge of Rachel's bed, Liz sank to her knees. Her black belt couldn't help her now. Her head throbbed with every pulse. A sledgehammer inside her head.

"I hadn't planned on this," Rachel said. "You never should have come back."

"Had to. Ben. Had to help Ben."

"Once again, you've made a mess. You never had any respect for me, for my work. The gardener found bits of those broken plates. How could you destroy those heirlooms?"

"Go to hell."

"Use the proper response. Yes, ma'am."

Her evil smile was magnified in Liz's distorted vision. She saw huge lips and teeth. Rachel's words echoed like she was speaking from inside a well.

"What are you going to do with me?"

"Everybody overheard your argument with Ben. He had a motive to get rid of you. Tonight, I'm going to make it look like you're his second victim."

She was going to die. Tonight. And Ben would be blamed.

Her eyes closed as she tumbled to the floor. Darkness overwhelmed her.

BEN ROSE FROM THE CHAIR behind his desk. He had to make up his mind and didn't have much time. Natalie would wake from her nap at any minute.

What the hell should he do about Liz?

She had come there under false pretenses. She had spied on him and lied to him. She had betrayed his trust.

Damn it, he was right to kick her off the premises. Keeping her around would have been a poor decision. The people closest to him had to be utterly trustworthy. He ran all his businesses that way, delegating to those who would act in his best interest. He needed loyal employees who were hard working and...

He smacked his fist on the hard surface of the desk. This wasn't about efficiency and business. This was about a small woman with wild hair and a great big heart. Her face appeared in his memory with her green eyes blazing. He heard echoes of laughter. He remembered her in that poorly fitted maid uniform, tending bar, posing as Charlene. He remembered her in his bed.

Damn it, he loved this woman. No matter what she'd done, he would not let her leave him.

He burst from the den and strode to the front of the house. She hadn't driven her own car and would have to get a ride back into town.

Near the front door, he encountered one of the security men. "Have you seen Liz?"

"Not recently."

"Check with the front gate. See if she's left."

The guard unclipped a cell phone-sized communication device from his belt and spoke into it. Turning back toward Ben, he shook his head. "The only person to come in during the past hour is Dr. Mancini."

That bastard. Ben knew exactly where to find him. He charged down the stairs to the lower level, where the doctor stood at the bar. As Ben approached, Mancini held up a tumbler of whiskey. "One more for the road."

"What the hell are you doing here?"

"Thought I'd pop in and say my good-byes." He adjusted his bow tie. "I won't be coming here every day. Not anymore."

"You got that right." Ben leaned his elbow on the bar. "Tell me, doc. How long have you been having an affair with Victoria?"

"A beautiful woman can make a man do foolish things. All she told me was that she needed money. Cash money. A lot of it. When I asked her why, she kissed me and I forgot about everything else."

Ben had a pretty fair idea of what he was talking about. "You provided Victoria with the cash to pay for a professional sniper."

"When I figured it out, she said she'd call him off. Then Ramon was killed."

Victoria was clever. If the investigation turned toward her, she could display her bank accounts and show that she hadn't made any sort of large withdrawal. She'd purposely protected herself and betrayed her lover.

Liz was nothing like Victoria. True, she'd come to the house on an undercover assignment, but she'd thought she was protecting Natalie from a drug addict father. Though she should have confided in him as soon as she'd known he was clean, he knew how hard it was to tell the truth when someone else would be hurt.

He wasn't about to give her a medal, but he could forgive.

Mancini straightened his shoulders. "I came here to apologize. I should have been more careful, should have asked more questions. And I promise you, Ben, I never did anything to hurt your grandfather."

"You kept him from getting the operation he needed."

"That wasn't me. I have professional ethics, and I knew I was out of my depth in treating a brain tumor. Time and again, I urged him to get a second opinion. As you know, Jerod is a stubborn old cuss. It wasn't until his vision started to go that—"

"Where's Liz?"

Taken aback, Mancini's eyes widened. "Liz? I haven't seen her."

"Did you know that she was a private investigator? Working for Victoria?"

"No." He downed the dregs of his whiskey. "Victoria is poison. The only thing she's ever done right is caring for Natalie. She loves that little girl."

Small reassurance, but Ben knew it was true. Being a good mother was Victoria's only positive attribute. "Agent Lattimer will be talking to you."

He poured another shot. "I'm almost ready for him."

Ben went back up the stairs to the kitchen, where Rachel and the chef were preparing dinner. "Rachel, have you seen Liz?"

Turning toward him with a chopping knife in hand, the big woman glowered. "I overheard your argument with her. She lied to you. If I were you, I'd want revenge."

"Do you know where she is?"

"I thought she was leaving."

He knew it wouldn't take Liz more than two minutes to pack up her things. Was she still upstairs in the tiny bedroom?

He ran up the stairs, two at a time. This house was too damned big. Liz could be out on the deck. She could have gone back down to the study. Could be anywhere.

In the narrow hallway on the third floor, he faced six closed doors, three on each side. He never came up here. Didn't even know which room Liz had been in.

He heard a faint tapping. It seemed to be coming from the door closest to him. "Liz?"

A whispered response. "Ben."

He tried the handle. Locked. "Liz, open the door."

Silence.

He jiggled the knob again. Something was wrong. Was she hurt? Adrenaline pumped through him. He hit the door with his shoulder. Once. Twice. On the third time, it crashed opened.

Liz was on the floor beside the door. She was bleeding from a head wound, gasping, struggling to move.

He knelt beside her, cradled her in his arms. Her eyelids fluttered. Her lips moved, trying to speak.

"It's all right," he said. "I'm here. I'll take care of you."

"It's Rachel," she said. "Look out."

A sound from the hallway alerted him. He turned in time to see the housekeeper brandishing a knife.

He sprang to his feet and faced her. She was a big woman. Big enough to have overpowered Charlene and carried her through the night. A monster. Rachel was the monster.

She slashed with the knife.

He easily sidestepped. "You know what, Rachel?"

"What?"

"You're fired."

When she raised her knife again, he slapped her hand aside and delivered a sharp jab to her jaw. She crashed to the floor with a loud thud.

He returned to Liz, gathered her close to him. With his free hand, he used his cell phone to call 9-1-1. Liz needed medical aid, and he sure as hell wasn't going to trust her care to Dr. Mancini.

With an effort, she lifted her hand and touched his cheek. "Love you." She forced the words out. "Ben I love you."

And he loved her, too. "I'll never let you go."

They would be together forever. He and Liz and Natalie. And Jerod. A real family.

Epilogue

Liz stepped onto the deck of Ben's fifty-foot yacht as they sailed the Strait of Juan de Fuca headed for the open seas beyond Washington state and Vancouver. The brisk autumn breeze swirled her long, white bridal gown. She'd never been comfortable in skirts, but this day she was willing to make an exception.

Natalie, also dressed in white, ran up to her. "You're so beautiful. Like a fairy princess."

She thought of Annette and her fantasies. "I'm not a princess. Just a woman."

A very happy woman. They'd closed up the house in Colorado and moved to Seattle for a fresh start. Ben's home in Washington wasn't huge or pretentious. No need for servants or housekeepers like Rachel. Just family. Their family.

She kissed Natalie on the top of her head and waved to Jerod, who sat waiting with his twelve-string guitar on his lap. He'd been practicing and played a version of the wedding march, mixed with half a dozen other tunes.

She linked arms with Harry Schooner, who looked very presentable in his black tuxedo. "Ready to give me away?"

"You're quite the door prize, Missy. Ben is a lucky man."

"Luck has nothing to do with it."

She gazed over the railing at the dark, mysterious waves, unable to comprehend exactly what had brought her to this point.

The inevitable dark thoughts intruded.

Victoria, Rachel and Dr. Mancini had all been brought to justice with varying results. Rachel had pleaded guilty and was serving a very long sentence. Likewise for Mancini, who would be incarcerated for two years for his unwitting part in Victoria's schemes. The lady herself— Ben's now ex-wife—was fighting the charges. Still awaiting trial.

As for Patrice and Monte? Liz began to smile again. Patrice had fulfilled her dream of being a talk show guest, partly because of the plump nudie photos. She'd taken a job as a spokeswoman for a weight-loss program.

Everything had worked itself out.

When they'd first moved to Seattle, Ben had wanted her to work for him, but Liz intended to set up her own practice after she finished up law school. There were a lot of people who needed legal help, people who couldn't afford a fancy law firm. And he'd agreed. He'd already started referring to her as the queen of pro bono.

Not a queen. Just a woman.

And he was just a man. As he stepped onto the deck in his tuxedo, he took her breath away. The most perfectly handsome man she'd ever seen.

She'd never thought she needed a man to take care of her, but she willingly gave herself to Ben. Heart and soul.

When Harry handed her off, she thought she might burst from sheer happiness. Ben's touch on her arm sent shivers through her. He leaned down and whispered in her ear, "Are you ready for this?"

More than ready. "Aye, matey."

* * * * *

*Don't miss Cassie Miles's upcoming books
of gripping romantic suspense later in 2008,
only from Harlequin Intrigue!*

Enjoy a sneak preview of
MATCHMAKING WITH A MISSION
by B.J. Daniels,
part of the WHITEHORSE, MONTANA *miniseries.*
Available from Harlequin Intrigue
in April 2008.

Nate Dempsey has returned to Whitehorse to uncover the truth about his past...

Nate sensed someone watching the house and looked out in surprise to see a woman astride a paint horse just on the other side of the fence. He quickly stepped back from the filthy second-floor window, although he doubted she could have seen him. Only a little of the June sun pierced the dirty glass to glow on the dust-coated floor at his feet as he waited a few heartbeats before he looked out again.

The place was so isolated he hadn't expected to see another soul. Like the front yard, the dirt road was waist-high with weeds. When he'd broken the lock on the back door, he'd had to kick aside a pile of rotten leaves that had blown in from last fall.

As he sneaked a look, he saw that she was still there, staring at the house in a way that unnerved him. He shielded his eyes from the glare of the sun off the dirty window and studied her, taking in her head of long blond hair that feathered out in the breeze from under her Western straw hat.

She wore a tan canvas jacket, jeans and boots. But it

was the way she sat astride the brown-and-white horse that nudged the memory.

He felt a chill as he realized he'd seen her before. In that very spot. She'd been just a kid then. A kid on a pretty paint horse. Not this one—the markings were different. Anyway, it couldn't have been the same horse, considering the last time he had seen her was more than twenty years ago. That horse would be dead by now.

His mind argued it probably wasn't even the same girl. But he knew better. It was the way she sat the horse, so at home in a saddle and secure in her world on the other side of that fence.

To the boy he'd been, she and her horse had represented freedom, a freedom he'd known he would never have—even after he escaped this house.

Nate saw her shift in the saddle, and for a moment he feared she planned to dismount and come toward the house. With Ellis Harper in his grave, there would be little to keep her away.

To his relief, she reined her horse around and rode back the way she'd come.

As he watched her ride away, he thought about the way she'd stared at the house—today and years ago. While the smartest thing she could do was to stay clear of this house, he had a feeling she'd be back.

Finding out her name should prove easy, since he figured she must live close by. As for her interest in Harper House... He would just have to make sure it didn't become a problem.

* * * * *

Be sure to look for
MATCHMAKING WITH A MISSION
and other suspenseful Harlequin Intrigue stories,
available in April
wherever books are sold.

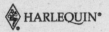

INTRIGUE

WHITEHORSE MONTANA

No matter how much Nate Dempsey's past haunted
him, McKenna Bailey couldn't keep him off her mind.
He'd returned to town to bury his troubled youth—
but she wouldn't stop pursuing him until he was
working on the ranch by her side.

Look for

MATCHMAKING WITH A MISSION

BY

B.J. DANIELS

*Available in April
wherever books are sold.*

the DEVIL'S footprints

Don't miss
the latest thriller from

AMANDA
STEVENS

On sale March 2008!

SAVE
$1.⁰⁰ off the purchase price of
THE DEVIL'S FOOTPRINTS
by Amanda Stevens.

Offer valid from March 1, 2008 to May 31, 2008. Redeemable at
participating retail outlets. Limit one coupon per purchase.

52608155

5 65373 00076 2 (8100) 0 11460

® and TM are trademarks owned and used by the trademark owner and/or its licensee.
℗ 2007 Harlequin Enterprises Limited

MAS2530CPN

HARLEQUIN

Super Romance

Celebrate the joys of motherhood!
In this collection of touching stories,
three women embrace their maternal
instincts in ways they hadn't expected.
And even more surprising is how true
love finds them.

Mothers of the Year

With stories by
Lori Handeland
Rebecca Winters
Anna DeStefano

*Look for Mothers of the Year,
available in April
wherever books are sold.*

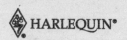

HARLEQUIN®

INTRIGUE

COMING NEXT MONTH

#1053 MATCHMAKING WITH A MISSION by B.J. Daniels
Whitehorse, Montana
No matter how much Nate Dempsey's past haunted him,
McKenna Bailey couldn't keep him off her mind. He'd returned to town
to bury his troubled youth—but she wouldn't stop pursuing him until
he was working the ranch by her side.

#1054 POSITIVE I.D. by Kathleen Long
The Body Hunters
In order to save his family from ruthless killers, Will Connor made the
ultimate sacrifice. Dying. Now facing the greatest challenge of his life,
Will must come out of hiding to rescue his captive wife, Maggie, and
protect his family when they need him the most.

#1055 72 HOURS by Dana Marton
Thriller
Parker McCall never stopped loving Kate Hamilton. So when rebels
attack the Russian embassy and take his ex-wife hostage, Parker gets
to prove it. Unsanctioned and nearly impossible, this mission's nothing
without showing Kate the man—the secret agent—he really is.

#1056 SILENT WITNESS by Leona Karr
With a killer hunting for the witness to his terrible crime, an entire
town was at stake. Detective Ryan Darnell had more than one life
to save—yet teacher Marian Richards may be the most valuable of
them all.

#1057 I'LL BE WATCHING YOU by Tracy Montoya
Adriana Torres was headed for heartbreak, and Detective Daniel Cardenas
was the last person she needed on her protection detail. Worse, Daniel
wouldn't let Adriana out of his sight—but neither would a killer who
everyone thought was dead.

#1058 LOVING THE ENEMY by Pat White
Kyle McKendrick vowed to protect Andrea Franks at all costs from the
rogue military faction hunting her. But Kyle was a mercenary, and the one
man she could never forgive. Even if everything she knew about him was
wrong.